First there was  QUASIMODO WA[...] Otherworld by acciden[...]

Then in RETURN OF BARMY JEFFERS he went back in desperation. What else could he do but dive into the Otherworld when a vampire grabbed him by the throat?

NOW he makes his most nightmarish trip of all when he pays a harmless visit to his friends in the Otherworld. But nobody has warned him about the bad-tempered monks with their shrinking potion or the golden spiders lurking in the lost tomb of Tarantulus.

Do you have the stamina to follow him on his latest journey?

About the Author

J. H. Brennan is one of those peculiar people who seem to
be living in several different worlds at once.

He has always been interested in magic, spells and
wizardry and has written a number of books on magic. He
is also the author of several Fantasy Role-Playing Games,
including the high successful *Grailquest* series published
by Armada.

Barmy Jeffers and the
Quasimodo Walk
Return of Barmy Jeffers and the
Quasimodo Walk

The Grailquest series

The Castle of Darkness
The Den of Dragons
The Gateway of Doom
Voyage of Terror
Kingdom of Horror
Realm of Chaos
Tomb of Nightmares
Legion of the Dead

Monster Horrorshow

Horror Classics

Dracula's Castle
The Curse of Frankenstein

J. H. Brennan

Barmy Jeffers and the Shrinking Potion

AN ARMADA ORIGINAL

First published in Armada 1989

Armada is an imprint of the Children's Division,
part of the Collins Publishing Group,
8 Grafton Street, London W1X 3LA

Printed and bound in Great Britain by
William Collins Sons & Co. Ltd, Glasgow

One

"Barnee!" Mrs Fogarty was shouting as impatience got the better of her. "*Barneeeeeeeeee!*"

But Barneeeeeeeeee ignored her, standing before the Möbius Warp like a sparrow fascinated by a snake. An internal hassle was going on so violently it threatened to end in a mental punch-up. Part of his head was telling him it must be a Möbius Warp. Another part insisted that it couldn't be, not when he was looking at a museum exhibit labelled *Mystery Artefact, Kan Tung Province of China, circa 758 BC*.

But *why* couldn't it be? By the look of this museum, the Chinese had invented everything else – why shouldn't they have invented Möbius Warps?

This hassle slid swiftly into another, just as violent. *Should he risk it? Should he Quasimodo Walk through the Möbius Warp*? He was assuming the apparatus still worked, of course, but he could think of absolutely no reason why it shouldn't. There were no moving parts to wear out, no fuel tanks to run dry, just the weird loop twisted so that it had only one side and hung so that somebody could walk through. Except, of course, that walking through was not enough. You had to *Quasimodo Walk*, to walk like a monster, otherwise the Warp just didn't work. If you *Quasimodo Walked*, however, you came out in the Otherworld. Somewhere . . .

Which was one of the problems. You knew you were going to come out in the Otherworld, but you never knew exactly *where* in the Otherworld. The first time Barmy had made the awesome journey he had emerged up a tree surrounded by wolves. The second time, he and his rotten little sister Lauren had Quasimodo Walked with two Otherworld friends, Rowan and Eynek. All four had found themselves in the stygian darkness of an ancient tomb. Theoretically, it was entirely possible to emerge in the depths of an ocean, or even confined by solid rock – circumstances to be avoided at all costs. Except there was no way you *could* avoid them: you took your chances.

He glanced again at the card on the exhibit. No wonder they labelled it a *Mystery Artefact*. Unless you knew about the Quasimodo Walk, that ghastly distortion of the human body that Barmy had invented to annoy Lauren when she was a baby, you could fiddle with the Warp for ever and the end result would be absolutely zilch. But should he Quasimodo Walk now?

"*Barneeeeeeeeeee!*"

She would, he suspected, go on shouting "*Barneee-eeeeee!*" for several hours if he did not rejoin the party. Alternatively, of course, she might decide to come and get him, a possibility to be feared more than an attack by ghouls. If she *did* come, she would seize his ear in a grip like pliers and march him back to his friends. The pain was not usually all that bad, but the humiliation would be indescribable.

There was one gigantic attraction to the Möbius Warp at that instant. If he got through, it would be without Lauren. On both previous visits to the Otherworld, she had come too. The first time she had followed after him, the second she had actually gone with him. This time, however, he would be alone . . . alone and *free*! He could hardly believe it. For the first time in years he would be able to

6

go where he wanted, do what he wanted, go out without any interference and settle his own fights. He might even manage to get a little closer to Aspen, with whom he now knew he was deeply in love. On his first visit to the Otherworld he had been too shy and stupid. On his second, Lauren and Aspen had become firm friends, effectively cutting him out of the picture. But against all that, there was the problem of his disappearance from the normal world. Mrs Fogarty was already shouting "*Barneeeeeeeeee!*" What would she be like if she stuck her head back into this room and found him gone?

Of course, it was entirely possible he might be gone and back before she even noticed. He had discovered time ran very differently in the Otherworld. It *seemed* the same while you were there, but you might remain for several weeks, then come back to discover that no more than a few hours – or sometimes even minutes – had passed. Kendar the Alchemist who specialized in Möbius Warps had once told him it just might be possible to return at a time a little *before* you actually went, thus making you wonder whether it was worth your while going in the first place. At the time, Barmy had found the concept bewildering. Now, however, it occurred to him that if he could manage to get back before he went, it would at least solve his problem with Mrs Fogarty, whatever the complications.

He glanced around. He was going to do it. He *knew* he was going to do it. But he still hesitated. Assuming he made the transition successfully – did not drown in the sea or suffocate in solid rock – and assuming he emerged somewhere near the Keep that protected civilization from the onslaught of the badlands monsters, what was he

7

going to tell his friends on the other side? What was he going to tell Ben and Lancie, Rowan, Aspen and Facecrusher? What was he going to tell Pendragon and the Amazing Presto? What excuse could he make for dropping in uninvited?

"What on *earth* is the matter with you?" Mrs Fogarty said angrily, bustling into the room and thereby sinking for all time Barmy's chances of slipping quietly through the Möbius Warp. "The whole party is waiting to get on. What are you doing anyway?" Her eyes glanced at the *Mystery Artefact* without the slightest indication of interest. She sniffed. "Wool-gathering, doubtless. Wool-*gathering*."

For the briefest instant, Barmy thought of making a break for the warp, hurling himself through, one foot dragging and his right shoulder up around his ear. But then common sense prevailed. "I'm sorry, Mrs Fogarty," he said politely. He felt depressed. He might never find another Möbius Warp his sister didn't know about and while he might manage to return to this one, his chances of finding himself alone with it again were somewhat limited.

"Come *along* then, Barney," Mrs Fogarty instructed irritably. She reached out to prod him with her rolled umbrella, one of her most infuriating habits.

"Coming, Mrs Fogarty," Barmy said. He followed her obediently out of the room, wondering not for the first time whether he had *really* done the things he remembered, whether he had *really* fought with ghouls and vampires, *really* conjured up a slith, *really* routed the dread Baron Tanaka, not once but twice. It didn't just seem to have been in some other world, it felt more like it was in some other lifetime, some other universe. Wherever it was, it was a long way away. He tried to

8

imagine himself dealing with Mrs Fogarty as he had dealt with certain enemies of the Keep. He tried to imagine himself sweeping aside her rolled umbrella with one flick of his sword and hissing grimly, "*Keep your brolly to yourself, woman, or I'll slit your gizzard soon as look at you!*" He tried to imagine it and couldn't.

"The wanderer returneth," Mrs Fogarty told the waiting class cheerfully. If she had one good point, it was that she never held a grudge, however long it took her to get her own way. She beamed at Barmy briefly, signalled the group to follow and marched off in the direction indicated by a sign which said:

AZTEC ROOMS

A fat boy called Harold Temple stopped her. "Please, Mrs Fogarty," he said, "I think I'm going to be sick."

It was fairly obvious to Barmy this was trouble. Harold had been eating more or less non-stop since they had boarded the coach at nine o'clock. His mother had supplied him with a flask of soup, a packet of sandwiches, some fruit, a tub of yoghurt, three bars of chocolate, a bag of boiled sweets and one of those thick, proprietary milk drinks which taste of synthetic strawberries. Now, Barmy noticed, there was little left but wrappings. If Harold was about to be sick, the result would be an avalanche.

But Mrs Fogarty was the sort of stoic who believed in willpower. "Nonsense, Harold!" she said briskly. "Just take a deep breath and think of something else!"

Harold could hold on no longer and poor Avril Harris was standing too close. Avril emitted a thin wail of dismay and disbelief. She stepped back abruptly and cannoned into Judith Forks, who lost her balance and

9

pulled down a display of Samurai armour in a vain attempt to stop herself from falling. A gauntlet struck a boy named Colm Callan who gasped in pain and then began to hurl abuse to no one in particular.

"Children, *please!*" exclaimed Mrs Fogarty in extreme exasperation, still blissfully unaware that while she might be dealing with a bunch of roughneck kids, she was certainly not dealing with anything as harmlessly innocent as children. She began to bustle towards Avril, dragging paper handkerchiefs from her handbag.

Barmy turned as if propelled by strings. He walked directly back to the room with the Chinese inventions. As he entered, he bent his left knee, curled his hands into claws, raised his right shoulder, trailed his right foot, shut his left eye, opened his right eye and curled his lips back in a soundless snarl. If there was anyone else inside the Chinese room, he did not see them. If Mrs Fogarty had noticed his departure, he did not care. If he was fated to end up in the ocean or in solid rock, it did not concern him.

Eyes shining, Barmy Jeffers Quasimodo Walked into the Möbius Warp.

Two

The first thing he felt was cold. It had been warm in the museum – and warm outside it, come to that – but here a chill wind cut through him like a knife, so that he huddled and shivered mindlessly. He was standing on a rocky plateau, wide enough to be some barren plain, while around him rose dark and bitter granite peaks. Nowhere within sight was there the least hint of vegetation; nor was there sign of animal life. He was alone in a world of icy rock.

Barmy glanced over his shoulder, but, as he had expected, the Möbius Warp was no longer there. The warps, natural or artificial, were strictly one-way affairs. They allowed you to pass between one world and the other, but they did not take you back. For the return trip, you found another Möbius Warp – or you didn't return.

He shivered again. The thought occurred that if he did not find shelter quickly, a return trip might be the least of his problems. He looked around. Those granite peaks extended into billow upon billow of yellow-purple cloud, a known feature of the Pileggi Mountains, parts of which were distinguished by volcanic activity which sprayed the dust that caused the coloration. He decided to walk. Even if it didn't get him anywhere, the movement might warm him up a little.

After Barmy had walked for twenty minutes, he was feeling a little more warm and a lot more depressed. He had reached one edge of the plateau and discovered his chances of getting down were limited to falling off a cliff.

The drop was absolutely sheer, with not so much as a foothold, let alone a path. How far it went he could not be absolutely sure – there was a rolling fog which effectively hid whatever lay below – but he could see enough to be sure it would kill him if he went over the side.

There was nothing else for it but to go back and seek another route. He turned and trudged disconsolately away from the edge. After five steps, something slid gently around his waist.

Barmy looked down in surprise. A suckered tentacle about the thickness of a good-sized tree root was in the process of twining itself around his body, but so carefully, so softly, it felt more like a caress than an attack. He was so taken aback, he stared at it while it made two more circuits of his body before he reached down to try to drag it off.

At once the tentacle tightened. "Help!" called Barmy, not very loudly since he was suddenly finding it difficult to breathe. He scrabbled at the increasing coils around him and found them supple as rubber, muscular and distinctly slimy. They were also roughly seven thousand times stronger than he was.

"Help!" Barmy called again, even more quietly this time. He found himself wondering not so much why he had Quasimodoed through the Möbius, as why he had been so stupid as to do it unprepared. He had entered the Otherworld in sweatshirt and jeans. He had no food, no compass, no change of underwear, no warmer clothes, no strong boots and he was without so much as a penknife for his personal protection. Could he not at least have taken a sword from the museum? He could, but he had not.

He was being dragged backwards.

Barmy glanced over his shoulder and immediately

wished he hadn't. Something out of his worst nightmares was looming up over the cliff edge, a creature so huge he had nothing to compare it with, except perhaps a whale. Although it was nothing like a whale. If the great waving tentacles were anything to go by, it was more like an octopus. Except that it was nothing like an octopus either, apart from the tentacles. It was patchy black in colour and mostly covered by a sort of writhing fur which gave the impression that it was a massive bed of maggots. In the centre of the writhing mass was a huge fanged mouth, topped by three of those multi-faceted eyes you see in blow-up pictures of a housefly. He counted nine tentacles – four anchoring the brute to the cliff, one around his waist, two more creeping across the rocky ground towards him and two waving in the air like reeds in a slow stream.

He panicked. "Help!" he screamed again, far louder this time despite his shortness of breath. He began to thrash about with a strength and energy born of desperation which, however, had not the slightest influence on the tentacle. As it wrapped around him, it slowly trapped his legs and turned him so that he could watch with horrified fascination as he was drawn closer and closer to the maw of the monster.

The two creeping tentacles had now reached him and were coiling around his body as gently as the first. Was there any way out of this? He had always accepted the possibility of being killed during an adventure. But he had imagined being killed in battle, sword in hand; being killed while performing some heroic deed. He had imagined his death in circumstances of glory, surrounded by his staunch and faithful friends. Walking through a Warp and straight down a monster's throat was definitely not in the scenario. But he seemed to have done it, more or less.

He was drawn to the edge of the cliff, then lifted some fifteen feet above the ground as easily as a child might lift a toy. The three great fly-eyes rolled in their sockets, their facets glinting in the light. He was drawn closer and could see reflected in those horrid orbs a thousand miniature images of himself. No matter which one of them you picked, he looked in deep trouble.

Attempting to think positive, Barmy concluded he was not being eaten, but rather being examined.

Prior to being eaten, the voice of honesty whispered in his ear.

The creature turned him this way and that. As he slowly felt himself turned the right way up, he suddenly noticed a second reflection in one of the monster's eyes.

Barmy twisted violently in sudden surging hope. He was right – there *had* been something! Walking jauntily across the plateau was a thin old man in a ragged cotton tunic and a pair of open, leather sandals. He carried a stout wooden staff, darkened and polished through years of use.

"Help!" Barmy squeaked. Then, more realistically, "Keep back!" The old man was obviously alone and certainly not warrior material. "Keep back, sir!" he called again. "You are in grave danger from this wretched monster!"

But the old fellow did not so much as hesitate in his stride. He walked directly to the cliff edge, nimbly brushing aside one questing tentacle with his staff, then called up firmly, "Put him down!"

"Sir!" called Barmy urgently, gripped by the sudden realization that the person fate had sent to rescue him was a raving lunatic. "Sir, this thing is very dangerous! It's too late to save me – you must get back!"

"Put him down I said, you great silly wallop!" the

14

old man screamed in irritation, waving his staff irascibly above his head.

And to Barmy's absolute astonishment, the coils around his body loosened and he was set down on the plateau as gently as a mother handling a new-born child.

Three

All the tentacles were withdrawing as the giant creature slid back into the abyss.

"How on earth did you do that?" asked Barmy in astonishment.

"Mmmm-do mm-what?"

"Drive off the monster, sir. I've never seen anything like it!"

"It's only a mm-baby," said the old man dismissively. "You weren't in any danger anyway – it-mm only eats fish."

"Then what was it doing with me in the air?" Barmy demanded. Now that the worst of the experience was over, he had broken out in a cold sweat and was shaking violently.

"Having a look at you, I expect," the old man said. "The young of any mm-species are curious about everything. You're young – you're probably curious about everything."

There was no arguing with that. When the worst of the sweating and shaking had subsided, Barmy said, "My name is Barney Jeffers, sir, and even if I was in no danger, I should like to thank you for resc – for getting me away from that creature."

"mm-krull," said the old man.

"Pardon?"

"It's mm-called a krull. The specimen you saw was quite young. Its parents would be roughly four times that size." Barmy closed his eyes and fought down an impulse to faint. "I'm mm-Brother Sunshine, by the way. Damn fool name, but the Abbot insisted on it," the old man added.

"*Brother* Sunshine," Barmy repeated. "You're a holy man?"

"Very," Sunshine said.

"A monk?" asked Barmy.

"That too."

"You must come from a monastery."

"Of mm-course I come from a monastery, you young idiot!" said Brother Sunshine who seemed to be working on a very short fuse. "Why else do you think I'd be mm-wandering around at fifteen thousand feet? Planting turnips, mmm? Weaving carpets, mmm? Only monks are mad enough to live like this. You should mm-mm-know that, even at your age."

"Can you give me food and shelter?" Barmy asked promptly. Monasteries were great places for a traveller. Most of them were obliged to take you in by the rules of their Order.

"Have you any money?" Sunshine asked.

A little taken aback, Barmy felt in his pocket. His fingers closed on something sticking to a bit of ancient gum, but it turned out to be nothing more valuable than a dog disc. Briefly he considered the advisability of trying to pass it off as foreign money, but his natural honesty got the better of him. "I'm afraid not," he said.

"Isn't that mm-typical!" said Brother Sunshine furiously. "I've been living in these mountains for close on mm-sixty years and I've never met a traveller with tuppence to rub together! But they all want food and mm-shelter. Oh

17

yes. And nothing but the best is good enough. But somebody has to pay. You realize that, don't you? *Somebody* has to pay. Fruit doesn't grow on trees, you know." He snorted.

"Does that mean you're not going to take me in?" Barmy asked.

"Did I say that? Did I say that? Did I? Well, *did* I?"

"No, not exactly, but –"

"There you are then!" Brother Sunshine exclaimed. "So just mm-keep quiet and follow me."

It turned out to be an utterly exhausting trek. Although Brother Sunshine looked as though he must be over eighty (and might even be well over ninety) he was as agile as a mountain goat and seemed impervious to cold or exhaustion. Barmy, by contrast, soon found his legs and back paining furiously and only a numbing chill made his sore feet bearable after the first mile.

They left the plateau, and, to Barmy's horror, struck out into the mountains themselves. The going which had been rough to begin with, now became a nightmare, with loose stones underfoot and the occasional sortie through narrow valleys rich with sulphurous fog from volcanic fumaroles. Eventually they reached a track and from then on the going was a little easier. It wound higher and higher into the mountains until they topped a rise and Brother Sunshine stopped abruptly.

"We've arrived," he said shortly.

Barmy caught up with him, more than a little out of breath. They were looking down into a shallow mountain valley. Their path led to the wooden gates of a rambling, ancient building, much of which appeared to be cut into the bedrock of the mountainside. The architecture

18

was unusual: all the buildings were flat-roofed and blocky, their design based on a series of squat cubes. Immediately outside the gates was an enormous iron bell, hung from a sturdy framework of time-blackened wood. With Barmy in tow, Brother Sunshine marched towards it and picked up a padded hammer almost too large for him to handle. Staggering a little, he struck the bell a resounding blow.

The note reverberated far across the mountains, echoing again and again until it seemed it must go on for ever. A small door set into the gateway opened abruptly and a tiny bald man in a sackcloth tunic emerged, eyes glinting angrily.

"Who's making that racket?" he demanded. "Oh, it's you, Sunshine – I might have known!"

"Of course it's me!" said Sunshine irritably. "What did you expect me to do – knock mm-politely on the gate?"

"Yes," snapped the little bald man. "Yes, that's exactly what I expected you to do. Not try to wake the dead by sounding our ceremonial bell."

"Knock mm-politely?" asked Brother Sunshine, reddening. "With somebody as deaf as you on duty at the door? We'd still be waiting here at mm-doomsday!"

"Excuse me, sir," Barmy said hurriedly, placing himself between the two monastic Brothers, "but I'm certain Brother Sunshine meant no harm at all in striking the bell. It's simply that I have requested the hospitality of your holy monastery and I expect he simply wanted to alert his colleagues to the presence of a guest."

"Have you any money?" asked the bald man promptly.

"No," Barmy said at once. He was getting a little fed up with monks who seemed interested in nothing other than loot.

"Doesn't matter," said the little man. "We'll feed and shelter you anyway. I'm Brother Moonbeam – it's a damn fool name, but the Abbot insisted."

"How do you do," said Barmy. "My name is Barney Jeffers."

Brother Moonbeam snorted and led the way through the door in the main gate.

Barmy stepped through into a courtyard which had once been flagged with natural stone slabs, expertly cut and dressed, but was now looking much the worse for wear with portions of it patched in rough cobbles. The yard was dominated by a massive polished statue of a robed ancient in cross-legged meditation pose. Before the statue a curl of incense smoke emerged from a small brass offering bowl.

Brothers Sunshine and Moonbeam bowed briefly to the statue and Barmy politely did the same. "Who is he?" Barmy asked quietly.

"That's the mm-Benign Immortal of the Saffron Robe," Brother Sunshine told him shortly. "He founded our Order two thousand seven hundred years ago."

"Oh," Barmy said. He noticed words cut into the plinth on which the statue stood, but they were in an ancient script which he found difficult to read. "What does that say?" he asked, pointing.

"*Serenity and Peace*, stupid boy!" translated Brother Moonbeam irritably. "Now get a move on. We haven't time to hang around here in the cold all day."

Barmy stifled a grin and followed the two bad-tempered monks out of the courtyard into the monastery itself.

Four

The scene in the communal dining hall was chaos. Barmy stopped dead at the door so that a monk cannoned into his back and hissed angrily, "Watch where you're going, Kipperfeet!" Barmy opened his mouth to protest, then shut it again. There were perhaps forty or fifty monks in the room, ranged around a massive scrubbed pine table, quarrelling, arguing, fighting and hurling abuse at one another. All were dressed in threadbare robes or tunics. Most were elderly. And every one seemed bad-tempered as a rattlesnake. Several were throwing food and one was clubbing another with a roll of bread.

There was a large water-colour portrait of the Benign Immortal of the Saffron Robe hung beside the door which Brother Sunshine bowed to briefly. "Serenity and peace," he muttered.

Barmy bowed as well. "Serenity and peace." A baked potato flew past his ear, but it seemed a random missile rather than a deliberate attack. "What's going on?" he asked.

"Lunch," said Brother Sunshine.

"Is it always like this?" Barmy asked, amazed.

"No, sometimes it gets rowdy."

Brother Sunshine waved his staff around until he cleared a space large enough to seat them both at the table. His age may have given him a certain authority, for those he whacked protested bitterly, but made no real attempt to hit him back. Barmy slid nervously on

21

to the bench, trying desperately to shrink into his skin so that he would appear as inconspicuous as possible. Sunshine climbed in beside him and began to pound the table with the handle of a fork, shouting "Food! Service! Guest here!"

A fat, extremely ugly monk in a greasy robe appeared carrying two wooden platters on each of which was set a bowl of soup, a slab of bread and a wedge of crumbly cheese. He slammed them down before Sunshine and Barmy so violently that the soup slopped over on to the bread.

"What's this?" asked Brother Sunshine at once. "What's this *muck*? Call this soup? I've seen more appetising mm-dishwater! And this cheese is mouldy."

Barmy tasted his food hesitantly and could find little problem with it. He was extremely hungry and began, unobtrusively, to eat.

"Good food!" growled the fat monk with a heavy accent. "You eat! Good food! I make!" He slapped his chest. "I make myself personally. Good soup, good bread, good cheese. After, Venerable Abbot wishes to meet guest."

"I'll need a saw to cut this bread," Sunshine complained.

"You are senile old maggot," said the fat monk. He sniffed. "After, Venerable Abbot wishes to eat guest for dessert."

Barmy stopped in mid-chew, but Brother Sunshine only said, "Wishes to eat dessert *with* our guest, you pig-ignorant tub of lard! Why won't you ever learn to talk properly?"

The fat monk shrugged, then smiled at Barmy and tapped his chest again. "Me Brother Snowdrop – damn

22

fool name, but Abbot insisted. You want good food, you come to me, eh?"

"Yes," Barmy nodded, "yes indeed."

By the time he had worked his way through lunch, Barmy was feeling substantially better, although the noise remained deafening and the odd missile still whizzed past his head.

"Don't hang around," said Brother Sunshine briskly. "The abbot doesn't like to be kept waiting. It makes him angry and you wouldn't mm-like him when he's angry."

Barmy hastily stood up.

"Let us out!" shrieked Brother Sunshine, belaying his monastic colleagues with his staff again. One fell backwards off the bench and Sunshine actually stepped on him as they made for the door. "Follow me, Honoured Guest," he called over his shoulder.

As the hubbub of the dining hall faded behind them, Barmy took time to consider his position. It was not, for once, all that bad. Of course, there was still the problem of crossing the wilderness – he couldn't imagine the monks would be all that keen to escort him all the way to the Keep – but he would deal with that problem when he came to it. In the short term, at least, it looked as though things were going his way.

They emerged into a cloister and from there to a small open courtyard, in the centre of which was a small stone bowl on a pedestal, in which had been set a beautifully laid-out miniature garden. Brother Sunshine stopped and bowed over it. "Serenity and peace," he intoned soberly, covering his mouth with his hand.

"Serenity and peace," Barmy echoed, bowing too. As he did so, a waft of pollen caught him in the nose so that

23

he sneezed explosively.

"You didn't cover your mouth, you stupid boy! You may have blown away our mm-founder, the Benign Immortal of the Saffron Robe," howled Sunshine. He whipped a large magnifying glass from the folds of his tunic and began to peer at sections of the miniature garden through it.

"You mean . . ." said Barmy. He gulped. ". . . his ashes are in the bowl?"

"Not his mm-ashes!" Brother Sunshine screamed. "*Him*!"

"Him?" asked Barmy, feeling stupid.

"Him!" shouted Brother Sunshine loudly. "Him! Are you deaf as well as thick? He *lives* there!" He was bending over, the magnifying glass pressed against one eye, examining the miniature landscape minutely.

"Lives . . .?" said Barmy slowly. "I thought you said he founded your Order two thousand seven hundred years ago? Or was that another Benign Immortal?"

"No, that was him," Sunshine muttered.

"But if he founded your Order, he must be dead for . . . for . . . for . . ."

"Of course he's not dead!" shouted Brother Sunshine. "He's an *Immortal* isn't he? Immortals don't die, you addle-headed twit – that's why they're called mm-Immortals!"

"You mean," said Barmy, who couldn't quite believe he was hearing this, "the Benign Immortal who founded your Order two thousand seven hundred years ago is *still alive*?"

"Yes," snapped Brother Sunshine. "That's what I mean. That's exactly what I mean."

"But why –?" Barmy interrupted. He started again.

24

"But how –?" And again: "Excuse me, Brother Sunshine, even if he *is* still alive, why would my sneezing in the bowl . . .?"

"Because he *lives* there! Don't you listen?"

"Brother Sunshine," said Barmy patiently, "that stone bowl is only forty centimetres in diameter – sixty at the most."

"He's mm-small!" screamed Brother Sunshine. "He's very small! He has to be to live in a bowl that size!" He straightened up and put away the magnifying glass, then fixed Barmy with a gimlet eye. "At least he *had* to be. There's no sign of him now, thanks to your stupid sneeze. I can tell you one thing, the Abbot's not going to like this, not one bit."

Five

The Abbot didn't.

"Serenity and peace, Abbot Nightshade," Brother Sunshine greeted him. "This young idiot has sneezed away the Benign Immortal of the Saffron Robe."

For a long moment there was silence. The Abbot was the largest man Barmy had ever seen, which may have explained why he got his way so easily when he insisted the monks adopt such foolish names. He was, on Barmy's estimation, just short of two and a half metres tall, muscled like a gorilla and sporting a long, drooping black moustache under a hooked nose and penetrating brown eyes.

"Pardon?" said the Abbot, at last allowing his thick, black eyebrows to crawl down his forehead into a lowering frown.

Sunshine explained with an economy of words which somehow made the situation even more devastating than it obviously was. For while Barmy did not believe a word of the nonsense about tiny Immortals, he suspected it might well be an article of faith in the monastery.

"So what do you want us to do about it, Venerable Abbot?" Brother Sunshine finished up. "Boil him in mm-oil or just beat him to death with clubs?"

"Here, just a minute –" Barmy put in hurriedly.

The huge Abbot silenced him with a glower, but turned to Sunshine before speaking directly to Barmy. "You're too quick off the mark, Brother Sunshine. Beating this young man to death will not recover our Immortal for us."

"No," muttered Sunshine, "but it would certainly be very gratifying."

"You go off now and meditate," the Abbot said.

"What about *him*?" asked Brother Sunshine eyeing Barmy suspiciously.

"You leave *him* to me."

"All right," muttered Brother Sunshine, backing out. "Just don't be too lenient on him. You're *always* far too lenient."

For a long moment Abbot Nightshade glared at Barmy, frowning, then abruptly held out a small wooden platter. "Would you like some candied orange sections?"

"Yes, thank you, sir," Barmy said, a little surprised. He took an orange section and, at a gesture from the Abbot, sat down at the table.

"You mustn't mind Sunshine," said the Abbot. "He's very bad-tempered like everybody over forty."

"What age are you, sir?" Barmy asked politely. He hated to think what life would be like if the Abbot became bad-tempered.

"Thirty-nine," said Nightshade. "I have been for years."

"I'm very sorry about the Benign Immortal," Barmy said between mouthfuls of the delicious candied orange. In the circumstances, he felt he had to say *something*.

"So you should be," growled the Abbot. "We've more than enough problems here without losing our Founder. What do you propose to do about it?"

Barmy opened his mouth, then shut it again. He was a bit at a loss to know what he *could* do about it.

"You'll have to get him back, you know," the Abbot said.

"Get him back?" Barmy echoed stupidly.

"You're the one who sneezed him away, so you're the one who has to get him back."

"Yes," said Barmy. "Yes, of course. Yes, certainly. I'll try – obviously I'll tr – With your permission, Your Abbotship, I'll go back to the basin right away and search most diligently. Most diligently. That's a promise."

The Abbot leaned forward, nodding and smiling, actions which made him look as friendly as a sabre-toothed tiger. "Yes, you will," he said. "You will search *most* diligently. But you will have to do better than just *trying* to find him. You will have to succeed."

"I will?" asked Barmy blankly.

Abbot Nightshade leaned back again and selected an orange segment which he viciously bit in half. He leaned his own head to one side and regarded Barmy strangely. "Have you noticed anything . . . peculiar about this monastery?" he asked. "Specifically, have you noticed anything . . . peculiar about the monks? Present company excepted, of course."

"Present company excepted, they all seem terribly bad-tempered," Barmy said.

"And why do you think that might be?" the Abbot asked.

Barmy hesitated. "They're all over forty . . .?"

"They are," said the Abbot, "which doesn't help. But that's not all of it. It's the fumes."

"The fumes?"

"From the volcanoes."

"From the volcanoes?"

"Are you making fun of me?" asked Abbot Nightshade ominously.

"No! No, of course not, sir. It's just that I don't quite understand . . ."

28

"The Pileggi Mountains are full of volcanic fumes," the Abbot said. "Most of them are just sulphur smoke and similar grot. But here around the monastery, you have a peculiar case of volcanic fume. No one's quite sure what's in it, but if you keep breathing it for more than three years at a stretch, it adds ten years to your lifespan, makes you immune to most diseases and shortens your temper. You can't escape it."

"Excuse me, sir, but how long have you lived here?"

"Twenty-two years," the Abbot said.

"You don't seem terribly bad-tempered to me," Barmy ventured.

"That's only because I have incredible self control," the Abbot told him blankly. "But take my word for it. If you don't find our Immortal, we will almost certainly run collectively amok and tear you limb from limb."

"I wouldn't want that to happen," Barmy said, venturing a sick smile.

"I'm sure you wouldn't and I'm sure it won't," the Abbot said. He stood up, towering over Barmy. "Come with me – it's time you were equipped."

"Equipped?" said Barmy, who was beginning to feel like Little Sir Echo.

"To search for the Immortal of the Saffron Robe," said the Abbot. "You don't think I'd let you go off on a dangerous job like that without the proper equipment, do you?"

Dangerous? thought Barmy. *What was dangerous about scrabbling through a miniature garden in a stone basin?* He followed the Abbot out of the room and through a series of gloomy, winding corridors. They stopped before a locked door which the Abbot opened with a wooden key. Inside, to Barmy's amazement, was an armoury.

29

He stared around at the most remarkable collection of weapons he had ever seen together in one place: swords of every shape and style; lances, pikes, halberds, a vast variety of spears; long bows, crossbows, slings, bolases and something that looked suspiciously like a woomera; knives, machetes, daggers, garottes, morning-stars, rice flails, bullwhips, clubs, maces, chain maces; leather armour, padded caps, helmets, chain mail, plate mail, gauntlets, greaves, breastplates . . . it went on and on and on.

"These are purely for the use of visitors," the Abbot explained.

Barmy glanced at him sideways, but did not push his luck by expressing disbelief. He was glad the Abbot kept the door locked – mealtime in a monastery of *armed* monks hardly bore thinking about. He stepped forward and hesitantly fingered a well-balanced broadsword.

"Take your pick," Abbot Nightshade encouraged. "Anything you want. Weapons, armour – you'll need all the help you can get."

Why? thought Barmy. *Why*? All the same, he began to buckle on some light but well-made armour. Past experience had taught him it did no harm at all to stay armed to the teeth in this alternative reality. And once he had successfully humoured the Abbot by searching the little basin, there was always the trek across the badlands to his friends in the Keep. All in all, he seemed to have run out of luck.

Armed to the teeth, Barmy followed the Abbot Nightshade back to his room. "Almost time," the Abbot told him cheerfully. He unstoppered a copper ewer and poured a generous goblet of reddish-purple liquid which Barmy took to be wine. "Sláinte!" he said, handing it across.

"I'm afraid I don't really drink alcoh –" Barmy began.

"Drink!" growled the Abbot.

Barmy drank. The wine (if it *was* wine) tasted musty with a bitter aftertaste and created an immediate bubble of warmth that rose from his stomach to envelop his head in an invisible cocoon of cotton wool. He found his perceptions changing, and at an alarmingly swift rate. Despite the chill of the air, what looked for all the world like a shimmering heat haze arose around him. He felt his limbs weaken, so that it was all he could do to hold himself upright. Had he been poisoned? Oddly enough, while he felt strange, he did not feel particularly ill, and there was no pain. He turned to the Abbot and found him grown monstrously large, his already massive frame distorted and exaggerated to truly gigantic proportions.

"What . . ." Barmy gasped. "What was that I just drank?"

"Shrinking potion," said the Abbot. "So you can go find our Benign Immortal of the Saffron Robe." His voice seemed to come from a great distance, high overhead.

Barmy swayed. He knew he must be hallucinating, but it all seemed terrifyingly real. Abbot Nightshade now looked larger than a mountain. The chairs and tables were artefacts out of a giant's kitchen.

A human hand the size of a house reached down towards him. He could feel a radiation of moist heat as the fingers closed around him. Then his balance went. He pitched forward on to firm, resilient flesh. The fingers curled into a funnel, trapping him beyond the slightest possiblity of escape. The giant thumb stopped up the only exit and suddenly his world was darkness.

31

Six

There was a period of confusion during which he might well have lost consciousness, for the next thing he knew he was lying on a flat rock overlooking a sea of jungle grass, each waving blade of which was at least as tall as he was, with some blades a good deal taller. Behind him, across a barren stretch of soil, lay a towering butte, porous with caves. To the east – or at least the direction he judged to be the east – he could see the gnarled trunks of quite gigantic trees.

He stood up, frowning. He was still in the badlands – everything about him was far too wild to belong to the cultivated north – but exactly where in the badlands he could not tell. Certainly it was nowhere he had been before and no familiar landmarks indicated it was anywhere he had ever heard of. He was seized by a sudden nostalgia for the Keep and all his friends.

Barmy pulled himself together and began to walk towards the giant trees. His first priority was to find out where he was. What he wanted was height – and the trees were the highest things in the whole neighbourhood.

When he reached the nearest tree he removed his armour and set it in a heap on the ground, placing his sword on top. In minutes he was swarming through the branches like a monkey. It was an easy climb, but long, so that he had to stop on several occasions to catch his breath and rest his aching muscles. For a while he began to imagine he would never reach the top, then suddenly he broke out into thin, chill sunlight. He propped his back against the bole and looked around.

Something about his surroundings was hauntingly familiar, as if he had seen it somewhere before. Which was, of course, quite impossible, since he knew he had never visited this area of badlands. Then he looked beyond his immediate environment and felt his muscles turn to water. For an instant, he could not comprehend what he was seeing. Then something clicked and the whole thing suddenly made sense. He was looking at an open courtyard of such gigantic proportions that it was utterly mind-blowing. More mind-blowing still was the human figure, taller than a mountain, now disappearing through a towering archway.

But most mind-blowing of all was the fact that he recognized the figure as *Abbot Nightshade*.

Barmy swallowed hard. He didn't want to believe it. He refused point-blank. But he had to believe it. The enormous tree he had just climbed with such massive effort was not an enormous tree at all but a *bonsai*. The immediate environment looked familiar because it *was* familiar: he had been staring down at it when the pollen made him sneeze. He was living in the ornamental basin with its miniature garden where the monks believed the Benign Immortal of the Saffron Robe resided. The courtyard was not gigantic, the Abbot no more enormous than he had ever been. Nothing had grown large: it was Barmy who had grown small. As near as he could judge, he was now only a little larger than a flea.

He began to climb down, slowly. This changed everything, of course. Up to now, he had assumed the business about the tiny Immortal was no more than silly superstition. But now he was forced to face up to the impossible:

33

he'd been shrunk!

He'd been shrunk!!! Not just his body, but his clothes, possessions, weapons and armour. It was impossible, incredible, but it had happened. He was now so tiny he would have to crane his neck and shout, just to talk to midgets. As he clambered down the branches of the giant tree – the *little* tree . . . the *miniature* tree – he began to feel very nervous. Life in the Otherworld was not exactly safe. On his first visit here, he had been treed by a pack of wolves. But at least he had had some opportunity to defend himself. What would happen to him if he met up with a wolfpack now? Or even a single wolf?

The thought occurred to him suddenly that a wolf – and just about any other dangerous animal or monster – would probably ignore him . . . if it even realized he was anywhere close by. As near as he could judge, he was not just little, he was nearly microscopic. As such, he posed no threat whatsoever to man or beast, and when you started to see things clearly, man or beast didn't pose much threat to him either. His worst peril would probably be someone stepping on him – and he should be able to avoid that fairly easily if he kept his wits about him.

Wasn't positive thinking wonderful? From the edge of panic, it had taken him to the realization that he was probably safer now than he had been at any time since he passed through the Möbius Warp.

He dropped out of the tree and found something horrible squatting on his little heap of sword and armour.

Barmy stared, his heart descending rapidly towards his boots. It was a lot smaller than a krull, but somehow far more alien and hence more terrifying. It stood – or rather crouched – about the size of a St Bernard dog, a jet-black creature from a science fiction nightmare with thin, hairy legs, multifaceted eyes, mandibles that looked as though they could crush stone and antennae that waved and probed in his direction.

Apart from the questing antennae, the thing was very still. Even its eyes did not appear to move, although that was possibly because they did not have to: when you had eyes cut like a gemstone, Barmy imagined, you could see just about everywhere at once.

What on earth was it? Cautiously, he reached down and slid an emergency dagger from his sock. He didn't really know if he was mad enough to tackle this thing in a fight, but he did know he wasn't mad enough to tackle it empty-handed.

He took a step towards it, more to find out what would happen than with any really aggressive intent.

Nothing happened. The thing remained exactly where it was, antennae moving in a slow dance.

Should he attack or was it just possible he might be able to *talk* to this thing?

"Hello," Barmy said, feeling very stupid. "My name is Barney Jeffers and you're sitting on my sword."

The thing raised one of its forelegs and waved at him.

Was it possible that it understood? Was the foreleg waving a signal? Did it communicate by sign language?

"Excuse me," Barmy said, feeling even more stupid, "but would you mind getting off my stuff, only I need to put on my armour."

The creature quivered. Barmy dropped instantly into a fighting crouch, dagger at the ready, certain he was the target of an impending attack. The creature spread concealed wings and flew away.

Barmy watched it go, the tension draining from him like water flowing from a jug. For the briefest instant he remained confused about what he was seeing, then suddenly it all came together and he realized what the creature was. A bug! A flying bug! The sort of garden pest his mother used to spray twice a year.

He ran to the pile and began to buckle on his armour as quickly as his shaking hands would let him. Next time, he knew, he might not be so lucky. Without arms and armour he was unlikely to survive for long.

As he armed himself, he pushed aside the nagging thought that even if he did survive the insects, he still had one huge problem: how to get back to his proper size again.

Seven

He began to explore the basin, a task which took him far longer than he would have thought possible. At the back of his mind was the notion that if he could only find the Benign Immortal of the Saffron Robe (in whom he now believed fervently) the ancient worthy might know how he could return to normal size. The Immortal had, after all, shrunk himself, so presumably he knew how to reverse the process.

Always assuming, of course, that Barmy hadn't killed him with the sneeze . . .

When he had finally explored most of the open space, he cut into what seemed like a jungle and there struck it lucky at once. In a smallish clearing he found a beautifully constructed Oriental-style house approached by a decorative bridge across an exquisite crystal-clear lake. He crossed and entered, finding clear signs of recent habitation, but no indication of anybody present now.

"Hello?" Barmy called. "Hello? Hello?" He moved from room to room with that uncomfortable feeling you always get in someone else's territory. Almost certainly this was the Immortal's home. There were several scrolls and books on philosophy, mysticism and monastic practice, a work on slith summoning, and an eccentric tome entitled *Astral Doorways*.

The Benign Immortal lived frugally – the only food Barmy found in the entire house was a little cooked rice and a jar of honey. He did not seem to sleep at all, since there was neither bedroom nor bed in the whole place. But despite a thorough exploration, there was no clue to where the Immortal might now be. Certainly he was not at home. Barmy began to wonder if he had sneezed him out of the basin altogether.

As he was leaving the house, a comforting thought struck Barmy. The Immortal, by all accounts, had lived in the basin for quite a long time. But his home was not defended. There was no moat, no portcullis, no castellated towers, no men-at-arms. The front door had actually been open and not one of the inner chambers had been locked. All of which plainly suggested the basin was a safe place to live.

By the time it started to get dark, he had explored all of the basin with the exception of the caves in the stone formation he had seen when he first arrived, and an area to the south which was a little difficult to reach. Since he did not fancy doing anything during the hours of darkness, he made his way back to the Immortal's house, closed the doors, lit a lamp, ate some of the rice and honey, then collected up as many cushions as he could to make a bed. He lay down and, rather to his surprise, slept like a baby.

The following morning he tackled the caves, bringing with him several torches from a storeroom at the rear of the Immortal's house. Since his whole experience equated caves with danger, he approached them with nervous caution, flaming torch in one hand and sword already drawn in the other. He quickly discovered that the caves and caverns interlinked, riddling the rock with a honeycomb of passages. Barmy had begun to relax totally and was actually tramping along whistling lightly when he walked into a spider's web.

Despite the difference in proportions he knew at once

what had trapped him – and recognized just as swiftly that he was in big trouble. The strands of the web were no thicker than his little finger, but stronger than steel hawsers. The web had been set near a cave entrance, cunningly angled so that it reflected little light. He had walked smack into it. The cross-cables were each coated in a viscous, rather pleasant-smelling substance which locked on to his breastplate and leggings like a metal weld and held him fast.

For a long moment he waited, listening. There was no trembling of the web that would have suggested the approach of the spider. He started to breathe again (carefully) and tried to think. His arms were free and he still had his sword at the ready. Could he cut the strands? More importantly, could he cut the strands quickly enough to escape before the spider came and ate him?

He considered the plan of action for all of fifteen seconds, then decided he had no other option. Bracing himself, he slashed once with the fine edge of his sword. It struck, rebounded and stuck tight to one of the horizontal cables. The web vibrated alarmingly.

Barmy distinctly sensed the answering vibrations as the spider started to investigate. He closed his eyes and prayed. After a moment, the vibrations stopped. Cautiously he looked around, but could see no sign of the spider.

After a moment, the vibrations started up again.

Barmy felt his mind go into overdrive. There had to be a way out of this mess. There *had* to be!

There wasn't. The vibrations stopped. He looked up to see a bloated shape looming out of the shadows. Luminescent eyes glowed hypnotically from the darkness. The spider was far larger than he was, only a matter of a few yards away. He did not know why it had stopped.

Why didn't it attack?

It occurred to him that he was still holding the flaming torch. Perhaps the insect, like so many creatures, was afraid of fire. It would certainly explain why it had not eaten him. He wondered if the web would burn. Cautiously he touched the torch to a strand and found it fireproof. His luck had run out. The spider lurched forward slightly. Without thought, Barmy transferred the torch to his other hand, then stuck it to the cross-cabling of the web so that it flamed between the spider and himself. The creature froze into immobility.

Barmy's convoluted little brain, fine-tuned by the rigours of so many desperate situations, presented him abruptly with a bright idea. Moving quickly, but taking great care not to touch the web with any portion of his exposed flesh, he began to unbuckle his armour.

In a moment he knew it was going to work. The breastplate fell away, still stuck to the web. Barmy sat down hard on the ground and began feverishly to remove the metal shin guards. The spider shot forward, panic at losing its prey presumably overcoming its natural fear of fire. A huge, hairy arm reached out for him. The strapping came free and Barmy threw himself backwards, half rolling out of reach. He came to his feet and ran, terror lending speed to his legs. Something told him the spider would not leave its web, but he could not be sure and he was taking absolutely no chances.

Without his torch, he was running blind, careering into the walls of the tunnel, scraping skin from his shoulder and arms. But he did not care. He was free and all that mattered was to put as much distance as possible between himself and that monstrous spider.

40

After a time he had to pause for breath. He forced the rasping of his lungs into stillness and listened. There was no sound of any pursuit. Barmy sighed. He had lost his armour and his most important weapons. He had lost his torch and his way. But for all that, things could have been a great deal worse. He started forward, tripped and fell heavily, striking his forehead a glancing blow against a rock and stunning himself momentarily. As he made to rise, shaking his head to clear it, something scuttled from the shadows and swept him off his feet. In seconds, he was surrounded by dark shapes and carried off at breathtaking speed along a gloomy tunnel.

Eight

They were ants! He was being carried by ants, each one larger than an Alsatian dog and – to judge by the ease with which they transported him – twice as strong.

A wave of pure panic swept over him so strongly that it left him shivering and weak. The big thing about ants was their co-operation. The creatures which had him now would never eat him, never harm him in any way. They would simply transport him to their anthill where other ants would wrap him up in some sort of sticky silk and hang him up to feed the children. Or maybe build him into a wall. Ants used anything they found, *everything* they found. And they had found him. All of a sudden the future did not look so rosy.

Now that his head was clearing, he tried to sit up. The ant that was carrying him sensed the movement, but did not try to stop him. Ants on either side, by contrast, reached across and held him firm. They had thin, wiry little arms which were nonetheless extremely strong.

Unable to do anything else, Barmy watched the tunnel ceiling speed past. He had begun to wonder where they were going when a sudden blaze of daylight half-blinded him. He was carried through grass – tall, waving fronds which turned the light a delicate green and looked nothing like grass as he remembered it – then through scrub under a forest of giant trees. An ant suddenly snapped off a segment of leaf and place it over him like a blanket, leaving his head free. Then he felt himself being tipped over and

42

realized he was being taken out of the basin. Barmy groaned. This was probably the worst experience of his entire life, a nightmare from which he could not waken. And he was helpless, utterly helpless, to do anything about it. Even his sword and armour were still sticking to that stupid spider's web.

The ants reached the bottom of the pedestal and started across the open courtyard. Barmy lost track of his surroundings after that, although it did seem to him they might have left the courtyard at some point. One thing was certain: they did not go inside the monastery, but rather remained in the open air. Eventually he found himself being pushed gently upright. He was standing before an earthwork dome. It took him no time at all to work out that the ants had brought him home.

He watched as one of the ants tugged open a sort of trapdoor to reveal a well-lit, inclined tunnel. Barmy frowned. If he had not known better, he would have thought the ants had somehow managed to invent electric light, but a closer look soon solved the puzzle. Set in wall niches at regular intervals along the length of the tunnel were tiny, immobile gloworms, each one producing a soft, bluish-white light which illuminated as effectively as any lamp.

He felt himself being pushed gently forward and entered the tunnel. He was still completely surrounded by ants so escape was out of the question, but he certainly preferred walking to being carried. The ants themselves surged forward, some splitting away to enter branch tunnels, but the main body escorted Barmy further and further, deeper and deeper into the hill. Everything seemed horribly well organized and busy.

The tunnel opened into a smallish chamber, which led

in turn to another and another. There was a different type of ant here, smaller and with slightly dissimilar markings. They ignored the newcomers, scurrying hither and thon like business executives with too much to do. Barmy and his large ant companions plunged into another tunnel. He wondered briefly how the creatures found their way. One tunnel looked much the same as any other. They were still descending.

For the first time, it struck Barmy that he was not at all nervous, although he certainly should have been. Had the ants drugged him? He had not been bitten or injected, but there was no doubt that the ants exuded a strange smell, pungent although by no means unpleasant. Was this aromatic fog a tranquillising mist? Was he continually breathing in some chemical which dampened down his aggression and with it his will to resist? He found the idea interesting.

It was a lot more than interesting – it was positively lethal! With a massive effort he tried to pull himself together – and failed abysmally. He was still placid, still calm. He even found himself grinning with amusement at his own failure.

Where was he going?

To see the Queen.

Barmy stopped dead, shocked out of his lethargy. An ant had spoken to him! He looked around to find out which one, but they were all ignoring him, scurrying here and there busily. Those behind pressed in on him so that he was forced to move on, heart pounding. An ant had spoken to him! More amazing still, it had spoken in English! Which ant? And how? Or was it an ant at all? Could there possibly be some other human in the anthill?

44

Maybe the drug they were using to calm him was sending him potty.

They entered a massive, high-ceilinged hall, swarming with ants. At the far end reclined a huge, monstrously fat creature he only just recognized as a disproportionately large ant. A constant stream of smaller ants surrounded it, carrying food, cleansing its body and carrying away smallish white spheres from a supply behind the giant insect.

The ants surrounding Barmy broke away, leaving him in splendid isolation. He felt compelled to step forward and did so, stopping only a few yards away from . . .

From the queen! This must be the queen! This was the way ants worked, wasn't it? The white spheres were eggs, laid by the queen in an almost constant stream and carried away to be hatched in some nursery chamber elsewhere.

Well done, Barmy – you worked that out very cleverly!

Barmy jumped. The voice again! He looked around him quickly, but there was no one, no one who could possibly –

Here, said the voice. *We are focused here!*

He felt compelled to turn again to look at the queen. Although it was absolutely impossible to be sure of the direction, some deep instinct insisted she was speaking to him.

Not me, said the voice. *Us!*

"Us?" echoed Barmy aloud.

We are the anthill, said the voice – and now he knew for certain it was sounding *inside* his head. *We speak through the queen, but she is no more than a part of us. We are the hill.*

This was not, Barmy thought, making a whole heap of sense.

45

It's quite simple really. The creatures you think of as ants are not individuals. They do not think for themselves and they do not act of their own will.

"Who's talking to me?" Barmy asked aloud.

We are, said the voice inside his head. *Now just listen! We are the entire ant colony. We think and act as one. A single ant is no more than a cell in our collective body. Our queen is an important organ, but no more.*

"But it's you who's talking to me, isn't it?" Barmy asked the queen. He had started to feel nervous again despite the drug.

If you want to believe she is talking to you, that's okay with us, the voice said. *It is wrong. It is stupid. But it is okay with us.*

Barmy took a deep breath. "All right," he said. "Why have you brought me here?" It was not a question he particularly wanted to ask, since he had a strong suspicion he was not going to like the answer.

We brought you here because there is someone it is important that you meet.

Someone? Some ant? If not the queen, then –?

The queen shifted her huge body slightly. From behind her, leaning on a twisted staff, limped the oldest human being Barmy had ever laid eyes on. He was so thin he was almost skeletal, so wrinkled there was not a square centimetre of exposed skin left unlined. But his eyes danced and glittered with an inner light and apart from the limp he had a sprightly air about him. He might have been an older brother of Brother Sunshine. A *considerably* older brother.

"What kept you?" he asked irritably. "I *hate* to be kept waiting."

Barmy blinked. The resemblance to the statue and the

portrait in the monastery was striking. He had no doubt at all that he was looking at the Benign Immortal of the Saffron Robe.

Nine

"You're friends with these *ants*?" Barmy asked, unable to keep the incredulity out of his voice.

"You haven't been listening, have you?" snapped the Benign Immortal. "I'm not friends with these ants. *Nobody's* friends with these ants. These ants aren't *capable* of making friends. I am friendly with the *anthill* and that's a very different story.

They were in an antechamber, (an *ant-e-chamber*, thought Barmy, who was feeling a shade hysterical) seated on quite a reasonable representation of chairs pulled up to quite a reasonable representation of a table, both apparently moulded from clay. Scurrying ants had brought them leaf plates of some sweetish substance with the consistency of porridge and were now carrying in nutshells filled with some white fluid.

"They keep aphids round the back and milk them every morning," the Benign Immortal explained, taking a nutshell and knocking back its contents with obvious enjoyment. "It's quite good if you don't think where it's come from."

Barmy sipped the milk cautiously. It had an unexpected citrus tang and was extremely refreshing.

"How . . .?" He was having trouble collecting his thoughts and started again. "How did you become friendly with the ants – with the anthill in the first place?" It was not a terribly predictable development. You didn't just walk up to an anthill and say: Hello, let's be friends.

"She's telepathic," said the Benign Immortal, as if that explained everything.

"She?"

"The hill's female, same as the queen."

"Why is the hill female?"

"Same reason ships are," said the Benign Immortal. "Now listen. I don't have all day to sit here talking about anthills. You're Barmy Jeffers, aren't you?"

Barmy blinked in surprise. "Yes," he admitted. "Yes, I am." He hesitated, then added, "Excuse me, sir, but how did you know?"

"The hill told me."

"How did it – how did *she* know?"

"You still aren't listening. You're the most cloth-eared individual it's been my misfortune to meet for the past five hundred years. I told you she was *telepathic*, didn't I? That means she can read your *mind*, doesn't it? What little there is of it," he muttered sourly.

"I don't think there's any need to be rude," Barmy said humpily. He was feeling quite fragile what with being shrunk and trapped by a spider and carried off by ants.

"Have I hurt your rotten feelings?" asked the Benign Immortal. "Tough. If you won't listen, you can't learn. Is it true you're an incredibly brave, skilled and experienced adventurer?"

"What?" asked Barmy, stunned.

"Deaf as well as thick," muttered the Benign Immortal. He raised his voice. "I said, is it true you are AN INCREDIBLY BRAVE, SKILLED AND EXPERIENCED ADVENTURER?"

"No," said Barmy. "No, of course not." He felt a little panic-stricken at the thought.

"So you haven't fought with ghouls?"

"Well, yes . . ."

"Or kept control of a runaway slith?"

"Yes, that too, but –"

"Or faced down Baron Tanaka not once, but twice?"

"Actually there were others with m–"

"I can't stand modesty," said the Benign Immortal. "It makes intelligent conversation quite impossible. I'm not modest, not in the least. I'm not stupid either. I need a good adventurer at the moment. Somebody with a lot of muscle and very little brains. Somebody who thinks with his glands."

Not at all sure the description fitted him – and even less sure he liked it if it did – Barmy asked, "Why?"

"To save the monastery, of course. You must have noticed how bad-tempered all the monks are. You don't think that's natural, do you? You're not one of those idiots who believes everybody over forty is bad-tempered?"

"Good heavens no," Barmy said hurriedly. "I thought it was the volcanic fumes."

The Benign Immortal frowned. "The what?"

"The volcanic fumes. Isn't it the volcanic fumes that makes them bad-tempered?"

"What a dumb idea!" exclaimed the Benign Immortal irritably. "Of course it's not the volcanic fumes, otherwise we'd all be bad-tempered. *I'd* be bad-tempered." He glared at Barmy. "It's money."

Every so often on adventures, Barmy found himself echoing things that people said, but turned around in the shape of a question. It made him feel really stupid and every time it happened, he determined he would never do it again.

"Money?" he echoed.

"Well, lack of it really," muttered the Benign Immortal.

"You must have noticed the tattered robes, the way the plaster flakes off the ceiling, the three-legged stools that started out as beds, the ghastly food . . ."

"I thought the food was quite good actually," Barmy said honestly.

"It's *muck*!" the Benign Immortal screamed. "Rubbish! Pigswill! And very badly cooked. Why do you think I live with ants?"

"I do agree with you about the rest," Barmy said placatingly. Then, to get the irritated ancient back on the rails he added, "It's all through lack of money, is it?"

"It's all through that villain Tarantulus!" growled the Benign Immortal. "You've heard of him, haven't you?"

As it happened, Barmy had. Tarantulus was an ancient king with a remarkable power over spiders, and had been dead several thousand years. The last time Barmy had visited the Otherworld, he had ended up briefly in Tarantulus' lost tomb.

"Yes, I have," he said. "But what has Tarantulus got to do with –"

"He stole our formula for alchemical gold."

Barmy knew he was going to do it again, but could not stop himself. "The formula for alchemical gold?" he echoed.

"We had a great monastery then," the Benign Immortal said nostalgically. "Decent buildings, decent food, decent clothes, best incense, new statues any time we wanted them. And when the money ran short, we just transmuted a bit of lead."

"Into gold?" asked Barmy. He had heard of alchemical transmutation, but never believed it possible.

"Into gold – of course into gold! Not much point in transmuting it into anything else."

51

"I understand," said Barmy quickly.

"Anyway," sighed the Benign Immortal, draining his shell of aphid milk, "Tarantulus stole the formula. Which made him rich and left us poor."

"You didn't keep a copy of the formula?" asked Barmy. It struck him that anybody who had discovered the formula for alchemical gold and only kept one copy must be feeble-minded.

"Keep a copy?" echoed the Benign Immortal. "Of course we didn't keep a copy – do you think we're feeble-minded? Start keeping copies and before you know, everybody has the secret. Next thing the market is flooded with gold, the price drops through the floor and you have galloping inflation. Don't you know *anything*? A copy indeed."

"I was only asking," Barmy said. He was beginning to feel as grumpy as the monks. He took a deep breath. "Let me get this straight. King Tarantulus stole your formula for alchemical gold?"

"Yes."

"And you were alive at the time?"

"Of course I was alive at the time! Do I look like a teenager?"

"No, sir, you don't," Barmy told him truthfully. He took another deep breath. "And having taken your formula, King Tarantulus got rich while your monastery got poor, and now you want the formula back – is that it?"

"Yes."

"Benign Immortal," Barmy said carefully, "King Tarantulus has been dead *for thousands of years*!"

"No sense rushing into things," the Benign Immortal said.

"But we don't even know where the formula is now," Barmy protested.

"It's in his tomb," said the Benign Immortal promptly. He leaned over, a sly look on his features. "And you know where the tomb is, don't you?"

"What makes you think that?" asked Barmy cautiously.

"*I told him so*," said the soprano voice of the anthill inside his head.

Barmy closed his eyes briefly. There were obviously no secrets in an anthill. He turned back to the Benign Immortal. "What makes you think I would be prepared to visit the Lost Tomb of Tarantulus just to recover your formula?"

The Benign Immortal grinned at him. "It's the only way you'll get back to your normal size."

Ten

"What you're looking for," the Benign Immortal emphasized, "is an emerald tablet."

"An emerald tablet," Barmy confirmed. He didn't care if he was repeating things like an idiot: the thought of getting back to normal size had cheered him up more than he would have imagined possible.

"It has the formula cut into it in Cyrillic lettering."

"Cyrillic?"

"Funny squiggly writing," said the Benign Immortal. "Don't worry about it."

"What happens if I get the wrong tablet?"

"You won't – it's a peculiar shade of green, like nothing you've ever seen before. You can't miss it. Now armour," continued the Benign Immortal. "Frankly I was a bit surprised you ventured out without any."

"I didn't," Barmy said. "But I had to leave it on a spider's web."

"Maybe just as well. I assume it was your usual run-of-the-mill metal – link mail or plate, something of that sort?"

"Plate. Your abbot gave it to me."

"I'll ask the hill to have the ants run you up something a bit more suitable." He scratched his nose. "In fact, I think I'll organize that now."

Although the Benign Immortal did not say anything and Barmy noticed no signal, a stream of ants poured into the chamber, chewing bits of leaf.

"You'd better stand up for the fitting," said the Benign Immortal. "Quickly now."

Barmy stood, watching the ants suspiciously. One scuttled over, reared and spat. A soggy piece of leaf splatted against Barmy's shirt. "Here!" he protested as he made to brush it off. "What do you think –"

But the Benign Immortal waved a hand at him furiously. "Stand still, can't you! How do you expect to be fitted if you won't –"

"It spat a bit of leaf at me!" Barmy told him, eyes wide. A second ant approached and spat another soggy piece of leaf so that it landed beside the first. "Look, that one's done it too–"

"It's your new *armour*," explained the Benign Immortal with heavy patience. "They're fitting your new *armour*!"

"Armour?" Barmy frowned.

Spit!

"They make it the same way they make their hills. When that stuff dries out, it will be hard as granite."

"I won't be able to *move*!" Barmy screamed.

"Yes, you will! Yes, you will! It's quite flexible, quite comfortable – a bit like rubber. But it's the best armour you'll ever wear."

Not having much alternative, Barmy endured. In minutes, his shirt was covered in a sticky mess of leaf. Several ants surrounded him and began to smooth it into shape, stretching the sticky mixture down his arms and legs until he felt like a human toffee apple. Then the ants retreated to make way for several new ones carrying large ferns, which they began to wave in unison.

"What –?"

"Just drying you out," the Benign Immortal reassured him.

He felt like a walking disaster, but to his great surprise the whole mess hardened into quite attractive body armour, darkened to a deep green hue. It was not, despite the Benign Immortal's promise, flexible as rubber, but it was a great deal more flexible than metal and remarkably comfortable to wear. He wondered if it would really stop a sword thrust.

Oh yes, quite easily, said the voice of the anthill in his head.

The Benign Immortal studied him, head cocked to one side. "You're not pretty, but you'll do." He sniffed. "Now, weapons. We don't have any, so you'll have to pick up another sword at the —"

We have his sword, the anthill said, as an individual ant scuttled in with the weapon across its back and deposited it at Barmy's feet. *We collected it from the spider's web*.

"Why, thank you," Barmy said, genuinely pleased. He took up the sword and swung it around a little the way people do. It felt good in his hand.

"You see," said the Benign Immortal. "A highly intelligent anthill. However, a sword may not be all that useful to you in the tomb — I understand the real danger lies as much with magic and traps as with straightforward physical attack . . ." He trailed off, thoughtfully.

"I don't suppose you could teach me a bit of magic?" Barmy asked. He rather fancied himself as a magician.

The Benign Immortal produced a piece of bamboo from a pocket in his robes and handed it across. Barmy looked at it curiously. It was about five centimetres long, partly plugged at one end with what looked like a wedge of ebony and cut with tiny holes arranged in a repeating diamond pattern. "What is it?" he asked.

56

"A telepathic whistle," said the Benign Immortal smugly. "The only one of its kind – I know, because I made it myself."

"What's it do?"

"It calls the colony."

"Colony?" Was he ever going to stop himself echoing what people said?

"The ant colony. Wherever you are, the colony will hear if you blow that whistle. It may even put you in touch with other colonies closer at hand: I don't really know. You'd be amazed how much help a friendly anthill can be if you get into trouble."

Barmy could well believe it. He placed the whistle to his lips and blew experimentally.

Hello, said the anthill cheerfully, even though no sound had emerged.

"See?" said the Benign Immortal. "Well now, it's about time you were off, don't you think?"

"Now?" Barmy asked.

"Why not now? You've got your armour and your sword and your telepathic whistle – what more do you want?"

"I can't tackle the tomb on my own!" Barmy exclaimed, surprised that anyone could live so long and still end up so stupid. "The point is," he said, "it will be difficult enough for a well-equipped party to survive in the Tomb of Tarantulus. If I went on my own, it would be quite impossible. So I have to get back to – Ben and Aspen, Rowan and all my friends. And I can't promise you anything, because I don't know if I can persuade them to come along –"

"I don't think you'll have any problems on that score," remarked the Benign Immortal.

57

As it happened, neither did Barmy. Almost all his friends in the Otherworld were mad enough to tackle anything that looked interesting and dangerous. At the end of Barmy's last adventure, the little thief Rowan had already been talking about a trip to the Lost Tomb. "Perhaps not," he admitted. "But I still have to get to my friends across the badlands and then there's –"

"No problem," said the Benign Immortal, "the ants will carry you. There are all sorts of underground ant tunnels between here and there. You could march it in a week, or the ants can carry you there in a couple of days."

Barmy blinked, wondering if he could be serious. He certainly *looked* serious. "What about getting back to my normal size?" he asked suspiciously.

"Just munch this when you get there," advised the Benign Immortal, holding out a nutshell filled with what looked like sticky porridge. "It's the stuff they feed the queen and look how big she's grown."

Eleven

It was difficult to judge perspective when he emerged from the tunnel. This was partly because of the sudden burst of sunlight, but mainly due to exhaustion. The untiring ants had carried him without pause for two whole days and several hours and while that sounded like an easy way to travel, he had found he could neither relax nor sleep. As a result he ended his journey feeling foggy, tired, sluggish, bewildered and grey.

The ants set him upright on what seemed to be a broad, barren plain, then disappeared back down their tunnel, pulling a little trapdoor closed behind them so that the entrance was not only sealed off, but totally disguised.

Barmy felt a sudden pang of desolation. He seemed to be the only human being for a thousand miles in any direction, with wasteland stretching out on three sides and a gloomy cliff-face looming on the fourth. He wondered, in sudden panic, if he could possibly be where he was supposed to be. And he wondered, too, at a substantially deeper level, if the little nutshell of sweet porridge was really going to reverse the effects of the abbot's shrinking potion.

Lacking a spoon, he scooped out some of the food with his fingers and ate it. Nothing happened. Since it tasted quite pleasant, he ate the rest. Still nothing happened. He tried not to panic – the Benign Immortal had warned him there would be a very noticeable delay – but panicked anyway. He was still panicking when the change overtook him.

It was not at all like the effects of the shrinking potion. It was much slower, for one thing, and quite painful for another. Worse still, he quickly discovered that the various parts of his body did not recover at the same rate.

The first thing to go was his left hand. It swelled abruptly to twice its size, double again, hesitated, then redoubled twice in the space of a few seconds. At this point, it became too heavy for his arm and fell with a peculiar splatting noise to the ground, where it anchored him firmly.

His right leg went next, growing like some demented tree-trunk until he was twisted as grotesquely as ever he had been in his famous Quasimodo Walk. Fortunately his left leg followed suit before he could do himself any permanent damage, but since his feet remained (for the moment) small, he fell over on his back.

He was thinking of getting up again when his head expanded. He lay there for nearly half a minute, big head, big legs, big hand, little body, little feet, before he felt his chest expanding like a balloon. His arms followed almost at once.

Feeling almost normal, he leaped up and promptly fell down again, since his feet were still pinheads. Fortunately they did not remain that way, but popped out at the end of his legs like a conjurer's rabbits. He stood again, more cautiously this time, carried out a quick mental tour of inspection and found himself bruised but reasonably intact. The food must have had a magical aspect to it, since his armour and sword had expanded with him.

He glanced around, amazed at how different the whole

scene looked now he was back to his normal size. The barren plain had vanished, converted to a bare patch on the grass and while the towering cliff still towered, it had now converted itself into the stone wall of the familiar Keep. He was, in fact, quite close to the Wilderness Gate, the precise spot where he had found himself when he emerged from the badlands on his very first visit to the Otherworld. Then he had had a hard time convincing the gatekeeper he should be admitted, but now at least he knew he could rely on a far warmer welcome. He was, after all, well known within the Keep.

He walked to the gate and knocked firmly. At once a small panel slid back and a pair of suspicious eyes looked out at him.

"Slope orf, Elf," a rough voice said.

Barmy groaned inwardly, seized by a horrid sensation of déjà vu. "I'm not an elf."

"You're green, ain't you? You're a little green man."

"I'm not a little green man – this is armour." He stifled a yawn. "Green armour."

"You're Irish, aren't you?" said the voice. "You're one of them there leprechauns."

Barmy wondered how on earth the gatekeeper had heard of Ireland, let alone of leprechauns, but he was far too tired to go into it. "I'm not Irish, I'm not a leprechaun; I'm Barney Jeffers and I want to come in."

"Who?" asked the voice.

"Barney Jeffers."

A peculiar gurgling sound emerged from behind the tightly-closed gate. It took Barmy a moment to recognize it for what it was – the gatekeeper laughing.

"Barmy Jeffers? Barmy Jeffers, eh? That's a good 'un! That's rich, that is! Barmy Jeffers is an *adventurer*!" hooted

61

the voice between chortles. "Barmy Jeffers is the *greatest adventurer the realm has ever knowed.* Barmy Jeffers is six foot one inch tall wiv blond hair and blue eyes –"

For the first time in his sleepy state, Barmy noticed that the small door in the entrance gate was ever so slightly ajar.

" – Barmy Jeffers is *muscular*! Barmy Jeffers is *handsome*! Barmy Jeffers mixes with Lady Facecrusher and the Bong and quality folk like that. Barmy Jeffers isn't an ugly little squat like –"

Barmy kicked the small door open and ran through to find the gatekeeper leaning nonchalantly against the gate, staring skywards, grinning stupidly and obviously taken completely by surprise. Barmy grabbed him by the lapels of his jerkin and pulled him forward so that their faces were just a few centimetres apart. "Ugly little squat?" he asked.

The gatekeeper swallowed. "Well, now I sees you in a better light –"

"I am," said Barmy slowly, "Barney Jeffers. *Mister* Jeffers to you." Tired as he was, his anger drained away and he let the man go. "Look," he said, "if you want identification, send for the Reverend Bong. He'll vouch for me."

But the gatekeeper was shaking his head. "Can't do. He's not in the Keep."

"Then send for Facecrusher. Or Aspen. Or Ben or the Amazing Presto or Pendragon – any one of them will tell you who I am."

But the gatekeeper was still shaking his head. "They're not in the Keep either."

"What, none of them?" He did not believe it.

"None of them," said the gatekeeper with an air of

62

finality. "They've gone off on an expedition to find the Lost Tomb of Tarantulus. Excepting for the Amazing Presto, that is. They put him in jail for letting loose another slith."

Barmy's tiredness evaporated instantly. "They've gone *where*?"

"To find the Lost Tomb of Tarantulus," the gatekeeper repeated. He squared his shoulders. "So, since you don't have nobody wot can speak for you, I am required in accordance with Section 42 sub-section 23 of the Gate-keeping Regulations to take you into custardy until such time –"

A monstrously large attack dog in a viciously spiked collar loped into the courtyard and bounded up to Barmy.

"Eynek!" Barmy screamed. He threw his arms around the dog's huge neck. "Eynek – it's good to see you!"

Slurp! Eynek's tongue licked his face.

"Come on, Eynek," Barmy said. "You lead me to Rowan so we can find out what's going on here."

"Just a minute!" the gatekeeper called officiously. "What about Section 42 sub-section 23 of the Gatekeeping Regulations?"

"He'll vouch for me!" grinned Barmy, jerking his thumb in Eynek's direction.

"He's a *dog*!" protested the gatekeeper.

"Grrr," said Eynek, placing one huge paw squarely on the man's chest.

"But his word is good enough for me," the gatekeeper concluded hurriedly.

Twelve

Had he not known better, Barmy might have suspected Eynek had got them both lost, for he led the way into a warren of alleyways and sidestreets that seemed gloomy even in broad daylight. But the huge dog pressed on confidently, plunging deeper and deeper into the most seedy district of the Keep until he flopped down before the doorway of a tall building that had seen better days. Above the lintel, in faded, peeling letters, appeared the legend

Guild of Thieves

Barmy knocked briskly on the oakwood door. It was opened at once by a wizened little man in a green doublet and brown breeches. "Good day, Venerable Doorkeeper," Barmy began. "I seek to –"

"Come in, young sir, come in!" exclaimed the little wizened man heartily, shaking hands. "You'll be a friend of Rowan's then?"

"That's right," Barmy said. "Is he here?"

"Just stepped out to the *Pint of Wallop* – Eynek knows the way."

"Grrr," Eynek confirmed. He turned and trotted off down a cobbled alley.

Barmy had followed him only a few hundred yards before the alley opened into a paved square and an unexpected riot. A small dun-clad figure burst out from a sidestreet at the other end of the square, hotly pursued by some twenty or more portly individuals dressed in merchant's garb, waving clubs and hurling abuse. From the tenor of their calls, they were intent on murder – or at very least grievous bodily harm. The small dun-clad figure was, without doubt, Rowan.

"What's going on?" Barmy asked in sudden alarm. But Eynek, who seemed to be much more accustomed to this sort of thing, was out of the alley like a rocket and bounding towards Rowan.

"Stop that man!" yelled a merchant, tripping over his brocade cloak. "He has my rings!"

"And my purse!" screamed another.

"And my braces!" roared a third, who was holding up his breeches as he ran.

Barmy reached instinctively for the sword, then decided he was not about to fight twenty maddened merchants who almost certainly had every right to beat the thieving Rowan. Instead he looked round for a possible escape route.

Meanwhile Eynek reached Rowan running at full pelt and Rowan swung on to his back like a horseman. Together they spun round and then they were off again only yards ahead of the merchant posse.

"Over here!" called Barmy. He had spotted a half-open gateway which might just help them all escape if Rowan and Eynek got far enough ahead of the merchants.

As it happened, he need not have worried himself unduly. Eynek put on a burst of speed that would have done justice to a racehorse and shot into the alley almost half a minute ahead of the rotund burghers.

"Quickly!" Barmy urged, pushing the gate. Rowan and

Eynek plunged through and Barmy pulled it shut again. He was walking innocently towards the mouth of the alley when the merchants rushed in.

"You there, young sir!" exclaimed the lead merchant breathlessly. "Have you seen an ugly little tortfeasor astride a giant dog?"

"Yes," said Barmy honestly. "They almost knocked me down."

"Which way did they go?"

"That way," Barmy told him, pointing.

"After them, men!" called the merchant and they all thundered off up the alley.

When they had disappeared, Barmy went back to open the gate.

"Hello, Barmy," Rowan said. "I see Eynek found you."

"Luckily for you by the looks of it."

Rowan slid from Eynek's back and embraced Barmy fondly. Although he was a full-grown man, he stood no taller than Barmy himself and might even have been a a centimetre or so shorter. He held Barmy at arm's length the better to look at him. "You seem healthy and fit. Is that armour?"

Barmy nodded. "Yes."

"Never seen green armour before. Where did you get it?"

"If I told you, you wouldn't believe me," Barmy said honestly. "But in any case it's a long story. Shouldn't we get out of here in case those merchants come back?"

"We'll go to the Guild House," Rowan said cheerfully, "and drink tea until the shouting has died down."

In the Guild House, two apprentice thieves (who might have been brother and sister by their looks) served them a pleasantly minty herbal tea and tried unsuccessfully to steal Rowan's purse. Barmy watched with relaxed amusement. With his toes toasting before a huge log fire, it felt good to be back.

"Is it true Lancie, Ben and Aspen and the others have gone to explore the Lost Tomb of Tarantulus?" he asked eventually.

"In a manner of speaking," Rowan said. "You see, Pendragon's leading the first leg of the expedition, so they're probably still arguing about what size of boat to use for the crossing." The Tomb, as they both knew, was on a small, mist-enshrouded island off the coast. "It's all your fault, you know, Barmy."

Barmy sipped his tea, which was having a distinctly tranquillizing effect after the earlier excitement. "How do you make that out, Rowan?"

"They're looking for you."

The tranquillizing effect evaporated. "They're what?"

"Well, when Lauren turned up with the news that you'd vanished from your own reality, Pendragon reckoned –"

"Just a minute," Barmy interrupted hurriedly. "Lauren's here? My *sister* Lauren's here?"

"Not here in the Keep," Rowan said, "but yes, here in our world. With the expedition, actually. You see, she agreed with Pendragon when he reckoned –"

"What's *Lauren* doing here?" He was appalled. The first time he had been really sure he'd sneaked away successfully, his rotten little sister had turned up in the same place.

"Looking for you," said Rowan impatiently. "You see, Pendragon's idea –"

"Looking for me?" Barmy echoed. "Why should she be looking for me? With the time difference between the two realities, I've probably only been gone about five minutes –"

"Apparently the difference in time isn't consistent," Rowan shrugged. "Sometimes it works one way, sometimes another." He obviously had little interest in the matter. "Anyway, the point is that when you disappeared, she assumed you'd Quasimodo Walked again and lashed up a quick Möbius Warp so she could come through and look after you –"

"*Look after* –?"

" – but when she reached the Keep –"

How was it Lauren could *lash up* a Möbius Warp and come directly to the Keep when Barmy found himself dumped in some godforsaken corner of the Pileggi Mountains? How was it Lauren always did things *right*? How was it –

" – and didn't find you here, she got her head together with Pendragon and decided you must have gone off to loot the Lost Tomb of Tarantulus –"

"Gone off to *what*?" exploded Barmy.

"Well, we did discuss the possibility, you may recall," Rowan put in mildly.

"We discussed the possibility that we might *all* go to explore the tomb, not that I should sneak off alone and –"

"Anyway, *I* didn't believe it," Rowan interrupted virtuously. "Even Barmy isn't dumb enough to tackle that place on his own, I told them. But they wouldn't listen. So Lauren and Pendragon put together a party and marched off into the sunset. Eynek and I stayed here. We thought you'd turn up eventually."

"Grrr," Eynek agreed, his head on his paws before the fire.

"Who's gone?" Barmy asked.

"The old team," Rowan said. "Lancie Bong, Ben, Aspen, Facecrusher, and Pendragon. And Lauren, of course.

68

She's actually the leader, but she's letting Pendragon think he is."

Barmy stared at him, wondering whether to be pleased or furious. If he was to keep his promise to the Benign Immortal of the Saffron Robe about his stupid emerald tablet, he had to go to the tomb eventually; and there was no question of going there alone – it was one of the most lethal places on the face of the earth. At the same time, he would have enjoyed an adventure – just one adventure – without his sister Lauren interfering.

After a moment, he said, "I'll have to go after them."

"Of course you will," Rowan agreed.

"I can't let them risk their lives looking for me when I'm not even there."

"Indeed you can't."

"Besides which, I promised somebody I'd get him something from the tomb."

"Of course you did."

Barmy frowned. "You think I've got an ulterior motive, don't you?"

"Not at all," said Rowan easily. He grinned. "Eynek will come with us: there's enough gold in that tomb for everybody."

Thirteen

They travelled in style to the coast in a smart horse-drawn carriage. When they arrived, Rowan wanted to steal a boat, but Barmy stopped him. In the end, they settled for hiring one from a villainous-looking seaman who reminded Barmy irresistibly of Long John Silver, despite his two good legs.

"By any chance," asked Barmy when negotiations were complete, "did you see anything of an adventure party which may have passed this way within the past few days?"

"Couple of women and the rest all men, ahr?" asked the seaman, rolling one eye alarmingly.

Barmy nodded. "Yes."

"Thin old swarb of a cleric, very tall, little poison dwarf and a blackguard of a paladin what looks heroic all the time, would ye say?"

"Yes," said Barmy.

"One of the women, young skivvy with gold hair, carrying a big stone ball on a chain with a little wooden handle on the end, ahr-har?"

"Yes, yes," said Barmy eagerly. "Have you seen them?"

"Can't remember," said the boatman blankly.

Eynek placed his face within a few centimetres of the man's nose. "Grrr," he said.

"Maybe this might aid your memory," said Rowan, pushing between the man and Eynek. He produced a leather purse and poured a steady stream of gold coins into the boatman's eager hand.

"By Gor, that it do, me hearty!" exclaimed the boatman greedily. "Them as what you do be enquiring after was here no more'n two days hence, and set sail yestere'en, late on, on accounting of the hasslin' and harguin' and suchlike, oh ahr."

"What did he say?" asked Barmy.

"They arrived a couple of days ago, but only sailed late yesterday because of some disagreement," Rowan translated. "We should be able to catch them up before they actually enter the tomb."

Whatever type of vessel the others had, Barmy and Rowan had hired a rowboat, which was slow and heavy going, since neither of them had much experience with oars. As the land disappeared from view, Barmy, who had lost the toss and taken the first shift at rowing, said, "You gave him an awful lot of money for the information, Rowan."

"I did," Rowan agreed. He held out a bulging leather purse. "Fortunately I stole it back again."

"Grrr," remarked Eynek with approval.

By the end of an hour, Barmy was beginning to wonder if they were going in the right direction. He knew almost nothing about navigation and Rowan seemed to be working by instinct, which did not exactly lead to a feeling of confidence. He cast his mind back to his last trip. He tried to remember what he had learned of the tomb and its surroundings.

It was not particularly difficult. Tarantulus was a king who had died several thousand years ago, having grown very rich through his ability to breed and train spiders (and, apparently, by stealing the formula for alchemical gold). His tomb was reputed to contain some of the most fabulous treasures in the history of the universe but was protected by a collection of mechanical traps and spells so lethal that no one who ventured into the tomb had ever come out alive.

Except, of course, that there was a strong probability that no one had ever ventured into the tomb at all – at least not before Barmy, Rowan, Eynek and Lauren stumbled on it through the Möbius Warp. The location of the tomb, a well-kept secret in Tarantulus' lifetime, had remained undiscovered for millennia. And with good reason: the tomb was actually situated on a small island totally hidden within a permanent fog-bank. The fog-bank appeared on sea charts as a place to be avoided. The island within it did not.

Which all came down to the fact that he should be looking out for a fog-bank. He glanced around him with disturbingly clear visibility.

"I hope you know where you're going, Rowan," he said uncertainly.

"Me?" said Rowan cheerfully. "I thought Eynek was navigating!"

Another hour and a half went by before Barmy, taking a fresh turn at the oars, suddenly felt himself begin to chill and glanced over his shoulder to discover he could see no more than a few yards ahead. "I think we've found the fog-bank," he told Rowan, who was lying in the bottom of the boat with his cap over his eyes.

"Well done, Eynek," Rowan said.

But whoever was really navigating, the congratulations were a little premature. Nearly three hours later, with night falling fast, they were still rowing around in the fog – an experience which shortened tempers considerably.

"We should have brought a compass with us," Barmy

complained. "Fancy coming out on a journey like this without a compass."

"Why didn't you buy one if you're so smart?" snapped Rowan. "Why leave everything to me?"

"Because you're the one with the money. Mainly other people's."

"Grrr," said Eynek, as much to himself as anybody else.

"I'm the one with money because I go out and earn it. Which is more than I can say for you."

"Earn it? You call stealing *earning*?"

"Of course I call –"

And so on, snapping and bickering for no better reason than the tightness of their nerves until the whole argument was stopped short by their running aground. Barmy, who was rowing at the time, did not realize what was happening straight away.

"There's something wrong with the water here," he said.

"What do you mean, something wrong with the water?"

"It's sort of solid," Barmy said, pulling vainly on the oars. "You don't think it's frozen, do you?"

"Not cold enough," Rowan frowned. He peered over the side, but could see nothing in the fog.

They might have discussed the problem for several hours, but Eynek solved it by leaping out of the boat. Barmy and Rowan looked at one another sheepishly, then followed. After only a few steps they emerged on to a wide beach of pale sand, fringed with heavy vegetation.

Out of the fog, it was growing dusk but still light enough to travel.

"Can you remember the way to the tomb?" Barmy asked.

"Not exactly, but it's a small island – we're bound

73

to stumble on to it eventually."

"Okay," said Barmy, "which direction shall we take?"

Before they could decide, Eynek bounded up excitedly. "Grrr," he said to Rowan.

"Eynek says he's found their scent."

"Whose scent?" Barmy asked.

"Ben and Lancie and the rest," Rowan grinned. "They can't be too far ahead of us."

"What are we waiting for?" asked Barmy. "Lead on Eynek!"

"Grrr," said Eynek, bounding off again, his nose twitching no more than a few centimetres from the ground.

Fourteen

They broke into a clearing and stopped. The huge pyra-midical structure of the Lost Tomb of Tarantulus loomed up before them, more or less as Barmy remembered it. The walls showed no sign of a door or any other opening. Nor was there any indication of the presence of their friends.

"Do you think they've gone inside?" Barmy asked, showing little imagination.

"Probably."

"Any idea how they got in?"

"No."

They looked at one another blankly. The last time they had Möbius walked into the tomb by accident, then opened up a passage from the inside (also more or less by accident) so their experience in finding secret entrances was somewhat limited.

Eynek lost some of his aimless look and began to follow what must have been a scent trail. For want of something better to do, Barmy and Rowan began determinedly to follow him. He led them round a corner of the tomb, stopped before a blank wall, sat down and howled.

"Has he found something?" Barmy asked. He had never heard Eynek howl before: it was a chilling sound.

"Either that or he's sitting on a thorn," Rowan frowned.

They trotted up and examined the wall. Barmy could see nothing unusual about it, but Rowan said suddenly,

"He's right – there's some sort of door here." He ran his hand across the surface. "The problem is," he added, as much to himself as anybody else, "persuading it to open . . ."

"Rowan . . ." Barmy said.

"What we have here," Rowan said, "won't be your ordinary run-of-the-mill secret door. This tomb –"

"Rowan . . ." Barmy said again.

" – is thousands of years old, so the builders would have used secret door techniques that have –"

"Rowan . . ." said Barmy.

" – been lost for centuries. What *is* it, Barmy?" Rowan said irritatedly.

Barmy pointed. A small group of very large, very muscular, very peculiar creatures had emerged from the jungle. They had fairly human bodies, but their faces were a sort of cross between people and pigs, with teeth growing upwards so prominently from the lower jaw that they were almost tusks. They carried spears held at the ready and wore heavy leather armour above thonged leggings and sandal-like footwear.

"What are they?" Barmy whispered. He had never seen anything quite so ugly in his life. Even ghouls looked like beauty-contest winners by comparison.

"Orcs," Rowan said.

"Orcs?" Barmy echoed. He frowned, then blinked. Like most of his friends, he had read *Lord of the Rings* and knew orcs were only a figment of Professor Tolkein's imagination. "Orcs aren't real," he told Rowan.

"Tell them that," Rowan said.

"But . . ." said Barmy. "But – but –"

"Don't panic," Rowan advised calmly. "It's only the local welcoming committee."

"They don't look very welcoming to me," muttered Barmy. He felt his hand creep towards his sword, moving of its own accord.

"You mustn't assume that just because someone looks different to you and me that he is necessarily an enemy," Rowan said. "There are always small cultural variations from one district to another, from one race to another."

"One of them's got a *bone* through his nose!" Bones through noses struck Barmy as a bit more than a cultural variation.

"Yes, I did notice that," said Rowan, "but it may be a sign of peace – you never can tell with orcs; sometimes they're perfectly civilized. Now you stay here and don't make a fuss and I shall make an attempt to establish communication." He raised one hand like a Red Indian in a B movie and strode towards the little group. "Greetings, Honourable Orcs!" he called.

Spears waved threateningly.

"Usfella, we come on from um big country, want see lovely island youfella livein, savvy, chop-chop?" Rowan said incomprehensibly, smiling.

One of the creatures hurled its spear, which missed Rowan by a whisker, but carried on to strike Barmy square on the right shoulder. To his surprised delight, the flexible green ant-armour deflected it completely.

"Naughty-naughty," Rowan said, wagging a warning finger and continuing to walk calmly towards the group. "Come on, Barmy – there aren't many of them!"

Barmy drew his sword and hurled himself forward. Eynek shot past him like a rocket, growling furiously. Rowan had his sword out and was moving towards one of the orcs.

With a slight rustling sound, several hundred more

77

of the hideous creatures stepped into the clearing. Most were armed and dressed like the others, but a few sported tattered doublet and hose which, apart from its condition, would not have looked out of place in the Keep. Several carried swords as well as or instead of spears, one or two had daggers also and Barmy even noticed one wielding a crossbow.

"Change of plan!" yelled Rowan, making an abrupt about-turn and taking to his heels.

"Oh good grief!" Barmy muttered and changed direction to follow him.

"Come on, Eynek!" Rowan called.

"Grr," muttered Eynek who was brave, but not stupid. He swerved around the nearest orc and bounded after Rowan.

There was a hissing noise as spears whizzed past them like a flight of angry serpents.

"What's the plan?" Barmy asked breathlessly as he caught up.

"Keep running," Rowan said.

They were not entirely surrounded, although it was a very close thing. The tomb blocked one avenue of escape while there were stretches of the jungle where the undergrowth was so dense they were obviously impassable. But if the situation was bad, it was not entirely hopeless.

"This way!" Barmy said, wheeling around.

"You're going towards them, you fool!"

It was true, but there was a gap in the pursuing horde. Barmy plunged towards it. Rowan must have seen it at the same time, for he followed despite his protest. A confused howl arose from the orcs as the three companions shot between them. Moments later they were running through the cool of the jungle canopy.

"Have you any idea how much trouble we're in?" asked Rowan.

"Grr."

"I wasn't talking to you."

Barmy did not bother to answer. Behind them he could hear the violent sounds of many bodies crashing through the vegetation. Their move had surprised the creatures only momentarily. They were in full pursuit again now and gaining all the time.

"Maybe we should split up," Rowan suggested. "They mightn't know which of us to follow."

"Maybe –" Barmy began, then stopped as the track they were on emerged abruptly into a broad clearing.

In the clearing was an orcen village, largely made from rubbish – mainly bits of old packing cases which must have come from some long-forgotten shipwreck. Around the village was drawn up an orcen army. Behind Barmy and Rowan, the sounds of the pursuing orcs drew closer by the second.

"This is another fine mess you've got me into," Rowan said.

It was not a slaughter, not even a decent fight, but in minutes they were overpowered and trussed up like three peculiar chickens. Barmy felt himself lifted off his feet and tied so that he was attached by his hands and feet to a long, stout pole. While he was still wondering what was going on, two burly females seized the pole and trotted off with him into the jungle.

Barmy glanced around to find Rowan and Eynek being carried beside him in similar fashion.

"You don't suppose they could be cooks?" asked Rowan, frowning.

As near as Barmy could tell, they were following the

same trail along which they had blundered only minutes earlier. And sure enough, only a short time later they emerged from the jungle into the clearing in front of the tomb.

"What do you think this is all about?" he asked.

"Grr," said Eynek.

"Search me," said Rowan. "Eynek doesn't know either," he added.

"It's some sort of religious ceremony," Barmy breathed, having been on the receiving end of several religious ceremonies in his day.

"You don't think we're to be sacrificed?" asked Rowan.

"Shouldn't be surprised," said Barmy far more calmly than he felt. When it had happened before, he had always been rescued in the nick of time, but he could not see who was available to rescue him on this occasion.

In the background, drums began to pound.

Barmy, Rowan and Eynek were carried to the base of the pyramid and dumped unceremoniously on the ground. The drums became louder and louder, faster and faster . . . then stopped altogether.

Barmy felt himself picked up again, still hanging from the pole. As he changed position he could see a whole series of ladders had been placed against the sloping sides of the tomb. Before he could orient himself properly, he found he was being carried upwards.

In other circumstances it would have been an incredible experience. As he swayed, he caught glimpses of the jungle canopy and the terrain beyond – a glistening river, a sweeping plain. Then, suddenly, all he could see was the dark mouth of a gloomy shaft which plunged into the tomb at a steep, downward angle.

"Here –" he protested in sudden alarm.

The drums began again and a huge shout erupted from the crowd below. Barmy felt the pole tilt. "Oh no!" he moaned.

But it was definitely *oh yes* as he was dumped, pole and all, to slide down the shaft into the very heart of Tarantulus' Lost Tomb.

Fifteen

He picked up a lot of speed in the shaft, but the ant armour stopped his getting skinned. For what seemed like minutes he slid through darkness, then noticed a dim light ahead before emerging abruptly over a pit which plunged downwards for a dizzying distance before it ended in a bed of vicious spikes, their tips coated with some sort of greenish ooze. Barmy caught his breath as he plunged over the edge and into the pit –

– only to be brought up short with a bone-jarring jerk as the pole to which he was tied jammed in the mouth of the shaft as he slid down. He swung slowly, like a pendulum, over the mouth of the pit.

Suspended in mid-air, Barmy wondered what his next move could be. On the face of it, his options were severely limited.

"Eeeeeeaaaaah!" *Crash*!!!

Barmy jerked and began to swing more wildly than before. The pole from which he was hanging creaked alarmingly, then shifted. Barmy felt his heart leap into his mouth, but the pole held. "What's going on?" he whispered.

"Barmy? Is that you, Barmy?" It was Rowan's voice, from somewhere inside the shaft.

"Rowan?"

"Grrrrrrrrrrrrrrrrrrrrrrrrrr!" *Craaaaash*!!!!

"Ooooooof!" Rowan gasped.

"Grr," Eynek's voice muttered.

"Rowan? What's going on, Rowan?" There was mayhem in the shaft and his pole was now creaking almost continuously, overlaid by a slow, splintering sound that chilled his blood.

"They dropped Eynek on top of me," Rowan said. "He weighs a ton."

"Grr," Eynek said.

"Can you see what's happening to my pole?" asked Barmy, reverting to his most immediate concern. If the pole snapped he was impaled on those spikes for sure.

"It's breaking," Rowan told him cheerfully. "It's jammed across the mouth of this shaft. It stopped me sliding any further, but with Eynek's weight on it now, it can't hold much longer. You just be patient, Barmy; when it breaks, we'll all be out of this stupid shaft."

The pole vibrated and the splintering sound grew louder.

"What are you doing, Rowan?" Barmy asked in sudden alarm.

"I can just about manage to kick it from this angle," Rowan said.

Barmy swallowed. "Rowan, I'm hanging over a pit full of poisoned spikes."

The vibration stopped. "Sorry," Rowan said.

"Any ideas, Rowan?" Barmy asked, not very hopefully.

Rowan said hesitantly, "This pit, Barmy – is there any chance of avoiding it if we fall?"

Barmy looked down. "Not if we fall. Not a chance, Rowan. If we were free and could jump, we should be able to miss it easily enough. There's a passage here that runs into the rest of the tomb."

"Anything in it?"

"Poisoned spikes – I told you!"

"I mean in the passage."

Barmy looked up and down the passage as far as he could see, which was not actually all that far. It was empty; nor could he make out any openings into side passages. "No, there's –"

The sudden jerk silenced him abruptly. It had followed a loud crack from his pole. After an anxious moment, Barmy whispered, "What happened?"

"Nothing."

"What *happened*, Rowan?"

"Your pole split a bit more," Rowan said. "Nothing to worry about – I'm almost free."

"Grr."

"So's Eynek – he's very good at chewing through things."

Barmy glanced back down into the pit, drawn by the same instinct that makes you keep sticking your tongue into an aching tooth. The stakes with the poison ooze terrified him, but there was something about them that puzzled him as well, although he could not quite decide what.

"Rowan?"

No answer.

"Rowan, do you know anything about pits?"

"Keep quiet, Barmy, I need to concentrate."

Barmy looked down again. Each spike was about a metre long, sharpened to a lethal point and fashioned, so far as he could judge, from wood. The green ooze, which he was convinced must be poison, covered about a third of each spike from the tip downwards. And it was definitely an ooze. It seemed to emerge, drop by drop, from the spikes thems–

No bodies!

There were no bodies, no skeletons, no bones! That's

what had been niggling at the back of his mind. If other victims had been thrown down the shaft into the pit and there to be impaled on the poisoned stakes, where were the bodies? There should have been the broken remains of every previous victim right there below him, cluttering up the pit. Even if the orcs had not made sacrifice for some time, there should at least have been skeletons, bones. But there was nothing.

"Rowan," Barmy said excitedly, "there aren't any bodies in the pit."

"Do shut it, Barmy, I'm nearly free!"

"You're not *listening*, Rowan. This is important. There are no *bodies* in the pit!"

"So . . .?" Rowan said.

"They must have made earlier sacrifices," said Barmy. "We can't have been the very first. They must have slid others down the shaft. But if they did and the others fell into the pit and got killed by the poison stakes, *where are the bodies*?"

"Carried off," said Rowan dismissively.

"Carried off?" Barmy echoed. His excitement turned to a creeping chill. "What do you mean carried off?"

"You know," Rowan said. "Rats. Ghouls. Monsters. Heaven knows there must be a dozen things in a tomb that could carry you off. And eat you," he added absently.

"You're not serious, Rowan. Are you?" Bad enough to fall helpless into a pit. Bad enough to be impaled by a spike. Bad enough to succumb to a green ooze of poison. But then to have your body carried off and eaten by a monster hardly bore thinking about.

"Grr!" exclaimed Eynek triumphantly.

"Eynek's free!" Rowan yelled. Then, more urgently, "Eynek, look out!"

85

There was a scuffling crash, a gasp from Rowan and a splintering sound louder than anything that had occurred before.

Barmy jolted and began to pendulum wildly over the mouth of the pit. "What's happening?" he screamed.

"Stupid dog fell on top of me again!" Rowan swore. "Get your foot out of my ear, Eynek!"

"Grr!" said Eynek wildly. The splintering noise was increasing alarmingly. "Rowan!" Barmy shouted. He felt his pole snap. He had just time to register the tangled shapes of Rowan and the giant Eynek popping from the mouth of the shaft like a cork from a bottle before all three of them plunged downwards into the pit on to the waiting stakes below.

Sixteen

Barmy's life turned into one of those nightmares you read about, but seldom actually experience. Time slowed to a snail's pace, so that he fell with agonizing slowness towards the sharpened spikes. As he fell he twisted, like an astronaut spinning gently in space. After an eternity, he could calculate with absolute certainty exactly where the spike woud pierce him.

It was ghastly. The spikes came closer and closer, growing larger and larger as they did so, until – in his new slow-motion world – he had dropped with a dreadful deliberation to little more than a yard from any one of them. He felt his body attempt to flinch away in that crazy instinct of self-preservation that always tries desperately, however unlikely it is to succeed. Then suddenly the slow motion snapped and he was plummeting towards the stakes at breakneck speed, nearing the stakes, reaching the stakes, falling on to the stakes –
which crumbled into dust beneath him!

He splatted on the floor of the pit. He was still there, spreadeagled and gasping, when Rowan fell on top of him; followed by Eynek, the barest instant later. He was so winded, he could not even howl in agony, although he felt most of his bones must be broken.

"Well, that wasn't as bad as it looked," remarked Rowan, rolling off him.

"Grr," Eynek agreed.

Barmy lay prostrate, unable to speak but groaning a

little. Then, since he was getting no sympathy, he pulled himself painfully to his feet. "That was –"

"Shh!"

"Pardon?"

"*Shhhh*!" said Rowan urgently. "There's something coming!"

Barmy shhhed. The lip of the pit was above his head so he could see nothing of the passageway, but all the same there was definitely something coming.

Something with a lot of legs.

All of a sudden everything Barmy had heard about the long-dead Tarantulus came flooding back to him. The king had been famed for his ability to breed spiders, including giant creatures no other webmaster could match. His tomb was famed for the lethal nature of its guardians. There was no chance, of course, that he could possibly have left some sort of giant spider which survived for thousands of years to . . .

Barmy pulled himself together. The thought was absolutely ridiculous. He shivered, remembering the giant spider which had trapped him in her web during the time he had been shrunk to ant size. But there was really nothing to worry about. Nothing at all.

Whatever it was that had a lot of legs was coming nearer.

Out of the corner of his eye, Barmy noted that the stake he had just demolished was growing back again to its original shape, as were a number of others he had flattened in his fall. It was an intriguing phenomenon, possibly due to fungi or bacteria. Obviously there had been real stakes set into the bottom of the pit at one time, but these had long since rotted. But the fungus or whatever it was seemed to mimic their shape, growing back again as soon as anybody destroyed it. Very weird. But at least the fungus only *looked* like stakes: it did you no harm at all when you fell in.

There was plenty of harm in whatever was approaching. It certainly had *a lot of legs*.

"What is it?" Barmy whispered.

"It sounds like a lot of people walking," answered Rowan.

It didn't sound in the least like a lot of people walking. To Barmy, it sounded exactly like something very large and very ugly crawling along on eight legs. Although Rowan was probably right: because it *couldn't* be what Barmy thought it was.

"What are we going to do?" he asked.

"The first thing is to get out of this pit," Rowan said. "I don't know who's coming, but I'd be happier if we weren't stuck down here when they arrive." He gripped Barmy's arm. "Come on, Eynek, give us a hand."

"No, just a minute –" Barmy began to protest. But like so many things in his life, his words came too late. With Rowan lifting and Eynek shoving, he found himself half thrown upwards.

He gripped the pit edge instinctively and pulled himself over, rolling on to all fours.

"Now you give me a hand," hissed Rowan's voice urgently. "We'll have to send a rope down for Eynek."

But Barmy was giving nobody a hand just at that moment. He was scrambling to his feet to meet the giant spider that – to meet the giant spi – to meet the giant –

"Hello, Barmy. What were you doing down that hole?"

It was Ben! He couldn't believe it, but it was Ben! Not a giant – not even a little – It was Ben! It was a whole lot of people as Rowan thought. It was Ben! It was Lancie!

It was Facecrusher! It was Pendragon! It was Aspen! It was . . .

Some of his excitement died. It was his rotten little sister Lauren, the torchlight glinting off her rimless glasses so she looked like something out of the Gestapo.

But even Lauren's presence could not dampen him completely. "Ben!" he exclaimed delightedly, throwing his arms around the dwarf. "Oh, Ben, it's good to see you!"

"It's good to see you, too, Barmy," Ben said stolidly. "Why are you wearing funny green armour?"

"To warn off funny green swords," put in the Reverend Lancelot Bong, grinning broadly. "You're looking well, Barmy!"

"So are you, Lancie, so are you! What on earth are *you* doing here?" he said turning to Lauren.

"Looking for you," said Lauren sharply. She had a talent for putting the boot in with the fewest possible words. "How *dare* you Quasimodo Walk without me! How *dare* you worry me like –"

"*Worry* you?" asked Barmy, genuinely surprised.

"Yes, worry me!" his sister told him. "Since you vanished on that stupid school outing everybody is almost out of their minds. I knew where you'd skived off to, of course, but it took me time to put a warp together and make the necessary calculations so I'd come through at the Keep. And then when I *did* get there, Lancie told me there hadn't been a sign of you. But I knew where you would be, you greedy pig: looting the tomb. I told them that. 'He'll be looting the Lost Tomb we found, I said, trying to keep all the best stuff for himself, sneaking –' "

"It wasn't like that!" Barmy said furiously. "It wasn't like that at all! I ended up in the Pileggi Mountains and got shrun –"

90

Surprisingly, it was Pendragon who cut in. "We know it wasn't like that, Barmy," he said reassuringly. "Lauren's just a bit upset."

Barmy waited for Lauren to savage him for interrupting, but to his surprise she said nothing. He wondered briefly if she was developing a thing about Pendragon, who was almost as handsome as he was pompous.

Aspen slid forward, her huge chained stone weapon slung carelessly over her right shoulder. "Hello, Barmy," she said simply, and kissed him on the cheek. He was still blushing furiously when Facecrusher came to hug him warmly.

"Are you all right?" she asked. "You're not injured?"

"No, I don't think so. Some orcs captured us and threw us down a shaft, but I'm all right except for bruises." A thought struck him and he asked, "Did you have any trouble with orcs?"

Facecrusher shook her head.

"They nearly killed us," Barmy said.

"You should have given them fudge," Ben told him. He blinked and added, "That's what we did."

Fudge? *Fudge*? Barmy let it go. Instead he said to no one in particular, "But what are you *doing* here?"

"Looking for you," said Lauren. "I told you that!"

"But since we *are* here," Lancelot Bong said in his best peacemaker voice, "we might as well have a little look round for the treasure, what-what?"

"Actually," Barmy said, remembering his pledge, "I sort of promised someone to keep an eye out for an emerald tablet . . ."

"That's good," Ben said. "We can make a plan in a minute." Ben loved plans.

"Tally-ho!" exclaimed the Bong. "Then let's be off!"

Rowan's voice floated up from somewhere below the level of their feet. "Not until you get me and Eynek out of this stupid hole!"

Seventeen

"We're here," said the Reverend Bong, pointing. They were squatting in a small, bare chamber some distance down the corridor from the pit and Lancie had produced a tattered sketch map drawn on parchment. As Barmy craned to see, he found it showed very little of the tomb.

"Who drew this?" he asked curiously.

"I did," said the Bong. "We've been wandering round for a bit looking for you, so I thought it made sense to draw a map in case we got lost and couldn't find our way out again."

Barmy squinted in the half-light. "Where *is* the way out?"

"It's not actually marked," said the Bong.

"No, I can see that. But where is it?"

Bong coughed. "As a matter of fact, none of us is exactly sure. Not *exactly*." He hesitated. "Well, not at all, really. The thing was, we didn't think of making a map until *after* we got lost."

"You mean we're stuck in this tomb and can't get out again?"

"I wouldn't say that," said the Bong. "You have to bear in mind we haven't been *trying* to get out. We've been looking for you. And looking around, so to speak."

"In case we found something," Ben explained helpfully.

"Which we did," Facecrusher said, smiling benignly.

"Which we did indeed," the Bong echoed. He stabbed his finger at a portion of the sketch map marked with a

93

large X. Although it was difficult to tell from Lancie's sketch, it seemed to indicate a circular chamber due south of where they were just now.

"What is it?" Barmy asked.

"I think we'd better show you," Lancelot said, standing up.

They approached the chamber via a narrow, dusty corridor where the natural luminescence dimmed progressively until Facecrusher was forced to light an extra torch. Eventually they stepped into a small, round room with a domed ceiling. Facecrusher held her torch high.

Although uncertain what he had been expecting, Barmy knew he had not been expecting *this*. The chamber was almost empty, bare of decoration and with no exit beyond that which they had used to enter. In the middle of the stone-flagged floor stood a huge wooden cube, set with dozens – perhaps hundreds – of little wooden knobs. For a moment, Barmy did not quite recognize what he was seeing, then realized the cube housed a multitude of drawers.

"What's inside?" he said. Subconsciously he had dropped his voice, possibly because of the expressions on his companions' faces.

"Take a look and see," the Bong invited smugly.

Barmy approached the cube cautiously, although he knew his friends would not willingly let him tackle anything dangerous. "Can you hold a torch over here?" he asked. Facecrusher moved silently beside him. He reached out and tugged at a drawer. It slid open easily. Inside, a two-inch diameter crystal sphere sparkled in the torchlight, throwing off tiny bursts of green fire. The smell of magic welled up out of the drawer like a heady perfume.

Barmy closed it and opened another. A concave black mirror rested on a velvet cushion. Stars twinkled in its depths.

Barmy opened a third drawer. An exquisite little ivory figurine of a sleek white cat crouched in the interior. A trick of the light made it seem to move its head, so that it stared up at him with luminous green eyes.

Barmy closed both drawers. "What is it?" he asked.

"There's something in every drawer," the Reverend Bong said excitedly. "Every one! Silk and vellum scrolls . . . ceramic dolls . . . ornamental knots . . . ebony tubes – you name it! Hundreds and hundreds of magical artefacts. They *are* magic, you know – no mistaking it. Even the drawers wouldn't have lasted this length of time without magical protection."

"But what do they *do*?" asked Barmy.

Aspen stepped forward. "We were rather hoping you could tell us, Barmy," she said lightly.

"Me?" Barmy echoed. "This is more the Amazing Presto's line, isn't it?"

"Definitely," said Lauren shortly. She sniffed. "Unfortunately he can't be with us."

"He called up another slith," Ben explained. "Only a little one, but it got loose and ate the mayor's cabbages." He blinked. "They put the Amazing Presto in jail and threw away the key."

"I heard he was in some sort of trouble," Barmy said. "All the same, what makes you think I'd know anything about these things?" He was, in fact, beginning to feel a little tense, as he usually did around magical stuff. He had a wealth of experience of how easily it went wrong.

"You did take magical training, Barmy," Facecrusher

said reasonably. "The Amazing Presto once told me you were a very apt pupil."

"Why me?" Barmy asked desperately. "Why not . . . why not . . ." He looked around for somebody else to throw to the wolves and found her. "Why not Lauren? She used to be Tanaka's War Witch! He thought she knew more magic than anybody in the islands!"

"Oh, for heaven's sake, Barney!" Lauren exclaimed. She pursed her lips, then said with heavy patience, "That wasn't magic – that was science! The Baron was not the most sophisticated human being in the universe. I just happened to have a few small examples of our own technology with me – the electric torch impressed him no end. But I never learned any magic the way you did, Barney: slith spells and so on." She glared. "Now stop being lazy and see if you can get some of those things to work!"

"But they –"

He was going to say they might be dangerous, but the Bong interrupted him before he could voice another protest. "You know that sketch map I just showed you, Barmy?"

"Yes."

"I don't know if you noticed how little there was of it . . ."

"I did, actually," Barmy said. "I thought you hadn't had the time to explore very much."

But the Bong was shaking his head. "That's all there is. That little bit we mapped is all there is of the tomb."

"But it can't be!" Barmy protested. "It doesn't show the bit we were in the last time we were here." Which was true, but what he really wanted to say was that it didn't show the way out – a point that had already been covered.

"Yes, I know," the Bong nodded. "Which means there must be far more to the tomb than we've found. Except that we can't get into it." The same thought must have struck him that had occurred to Barmy, for he added, "Or out of it, come to that, what?"

"Have you searched for secret doors?" asked Rowan.

"Of course we've searched for secret doors!" said Lauren so sharply that Eynek moved between her and Rowan. But Barmy, who had known her longer than the rest recognized the tone was more suppressed panic than anger. Lauren was never entirely happy in enclosed spaces. Enclosed spaces *where she did not know the way out* made her very nervous indeed.

"There aren't any secret doors, Rowan," Ben said earnestly. "We looked everywhere. The only way out is that shaft you and Barmy and Eynek came in through and it's too slippery to climb."

"But you didn't come in that way, did you?" Barmy asked. "I mean you weren't dropped in by the orcs; you gave them fudge or something, didn't you?"

The Bong nodded. "Yes, that's true. We came in by way of a descending passageway that opened into the north face of the pyramid. The thing is, it closed up after us."

"It must have sealed itself off by magic," Aspen said coolly.

"You mean the magic of Tarantulus is still working after all this time?" Barmy said. He realized it was a stupid question even as he voiced it. The cube in front of him was jam-packed with magic, still humming and sparkling as fresh as the day the spells were cast. Tarantulus must have been an expert on more than spiders.

"What we think," said the Reverend Bong cheerfully, "is that the key into the rest of the tomb –"

"And getting *out* of the tomb," put in Lauren.

"– must be one of those magical artefacts," the Bong concluded. "So naturally we thought it would be a good idea if you . . ." He shrugged, letting the sentence hang.

"Messed about with them," Barmy muttered sourly.

"That's right," Ben said. He looked at Barmy seriously. "Because if you don't, I think we may be trapped here until we all die of starvation."

Eighteen

Barmy began to open the drawers in sequence and lay out their contents in a careful grid pattern on the floor. He did not know what he was doing, but experience had taught him that if you proceeded methodically, people often mistook this for expertise.

There was no doubt the artefacts were magic. All had that faint but unmistakable scent of incense and most gave a buzz when touched. Their variety was staggering. As each item emerged from the honeycomb cube, the atmosphere of magic in the chamber increased noticeably, with inevitable results. Lancelot and Ben were fidgeting nervously. Aspen, Lauren and Facecrusher were pacing up and down. Rowan was huddled in a corner, eyes bright, and Eynek had to keep slipping out into the corridor on account of the excitement.

It took a long time, but eventually the drawers were empty, their contents laid out neatly on the floor, humming and sparkling. It was the moment of truth, since Barmy had not the least idea what to do next.

"Go on then," Ben urged encouragingly.

Barmy reached for a small ebony cube with a different pattern inlaid on each of its six sides. Of all the artefacts laid out, it was the one which came closest to familiarity; not because he had seen anything like it before, but rather because he seemed to remember the Amazing Presto once described something similar that was produced at a Wizards' Convention. Cautiously he rolled it on the flagstones like a die.

Sheets of shimmering multicoloured lights flared out and the chamber was filled with perfume as patterns whirled and danced together in the air. The display lasted for perhaps half a minute, then died.

After a moment Pendragon asked, "Is that it?"

"I think it was very pretty," Lauren said loyally. She might criticize Barmy and fancy Pendragon, but the habit of sticking up for her big brother in face of the mildest criticism was obviously one she was not prepared to break.

"Yes," Aspen said. "Yes, it was."

"What are you going to do next, Barmy?" Ben asked excitedly. Before Barmy could stop him, he swooped on a slim, hollow tube about twenty centimetres long and handed it across. "What does this do, Barmy?"

The tube, which seemed to be made from horn, was tapered at one end and stoppered with a cork at the other. There were smallish holes along part of its length, which made Barmy think it might be a musical instrument: a whistle, or a flute of some description. He closed two of the holes with his fingers and blew down it experimentally. No sound emerged, but he got a mouthful of orange juice.

He stopped coughing eventually and tried again, this time with his fingers in different positions. It filled his mouth with a plummy wine. Barmy swallowed without thinking and felt a warm glow spreading from his stomach. "It pours drinks," he said unwisely and found himself instantly surrounded by his companions holding goblets produced from thin air.

"Eynek really likes Bourbon," Rowan said, but Barmy ignored him. He moved from goblet to goblet, shifting his fingers to change the liquid poured into each. There were a variety of fruit juices, along with the plummy wine, a heavy, sweetish ale, a honey drink that might have been mead and something that smelt like cherry brandy.

"I don't suppose you could persuade it to dispense a drop of port?" suggested Lancie, but in the event ended up with a goblet of fizzy lemon.

It was a merry little interlude which came to an end far too quickly as far as Barmy was concerned.

"Do something else, Barmy," Ben urged in what was beginning to sound like a voice of cheerful doom. "See if you can get us into the rest of the tomb."

"I'm not sure –"

But before he could finish, the Bong had lifted a little twisted ebony wand. "What about this thing, what? Looks interesting, don't you think, Barm –"

A fork of lightning snaked from the end of the wand to gouge bits out of the nearest wall with a crackling sound that was nearly deafening. The chamber filled at once with the smell of ozone. With a fine-honed instinct born of many battles, the party members – Barmy included – flung themselves flat on the ground.

"What?" asked the Bong, confused. He tilted the wand, the better to examine it, and gouged a crater in the ceiling. A spiderweb of cracks formed under the impact of the continuous lightning and bits began to fall in a shower of rubble that threatened to bring down the entire roof.

"Put it down!" screamed Pendragon.

"Drop it!" Aspen yelled. "Put the wand down, Lancie!"

"Let go the wand!!" bellowed Facecrusher.

But it was Ben who resolved the crisis by creeping up behind the Bong and striking him sharply in the small of the back. The wand fell to the ground and ceased to spit lightning. "Why did you do that?" the Reverend Bong demanded, turning to frown down at Ben.

101

"You had become a menace to society, Lancie," Ben said stolidly.

"Don't touch!" Barmy called, scrambling to his feet. "Don't touch . . . *anything*." It had been like this for as long as he could remember. However careful you were personally, there was always somebody on hand to provoke a disaster. Usually Lancie. He looked over to Lauren, wondering if he dared enlist her help. But he didn't quite know what help he needed. Maybe he should just refuse to play around with any more of the artefacts, but then, as Ben had remarked earlier, they would be trapped in this one small section of the tomb.

"Maybe you could use that," Ben suggested. He was pointing at another wand, longer, straighter and made from iron this time, but was careful not to touch it.

Barmy almost ignored him, then some instinct persuaded him to ask, "You don't happen to know what it is, do you?"

"Oh yes," Ben nodded, "it's a dwarven Wand of Digging."

"A dwarven Wand of –" Barmy stopped himself going into echo mode and said instead, "You don't happen to know what it does?"

"Oh yes," said Ben. "It digs holes." He blinked, then added, "As far as you want, through anything."

If it dug holes as far as you wanted through anything, then it could dig them out of this section of the tomb. Provided the hole was big enough.

"How big holes?" he asked cautiously.

"As big as you like, Barmy," Ben said. "You can use it for tunnelling if you want."

Barmy licked his lips. It looked as if they might, just *might*, be out of the woods. But you never could tell when you were dealing with Ben. "I don't suppose you, ah, know *how* to use it, Ben?"

"Oh yes," Ben said.

The silence stretched while Barmy fought back an urge to seize him by the throat. Eventually, politely, he asked, "How do you use it, Ben?"

"You point it at where you want to dig, Barmy," Ben said, "and you make sure there's nobody standing in front and then you squeeze the end you're holding three times and on the third time a big beam of black light comes out and digs the hole. It's very easy once you get the hang of it."

"All right," Barmy said. "Everybody stand back." He swung the wand towards the nearest wall. If he managed to cut a hole, it would only let them into the corridor, but he wanted to experiment with something simple before starting into anything important.

"Are you sure you know what you're doing?" Lauren asked.

He did not, of course, but he wasn't going to admit it. "You just stand clear, Lauren," he told her sourly. She did, as did the others. Barmy glanced across to find them all cowering against the most distant wall. "Thanks for the vote of confidence," he muttered. He pointed the wand at the wall. "Like this, Ben?"

"That's right, Barmy."

"And squeeze the end?"

"That's right, Barmy."

"Three times, is it?"

"That's right, Barmy."

He squeezed the end three times and nothing happened. He squeezed again in another sequence of three. Still nothing happened. "Nothing's happening, Ben."

"It only works for dwarves," Ben said.

Barmy savagely suppressed an eruption of fury. Very calmly, very quietly, he handed the wand across. "You try it, Ben."

"All right, Barmy." He waved the wand around, as if testing its balance.

"Careful, Ben," Aspen warned.

"It's quite safe, Aspirin, unless you squeeze it three times," Ben said. "But I will just point it at the wall the way Barmy did by way of demonstration." He pointed at the wall. "Now," he said, "you squeeze three times. One . . . two . . . thr –"

The wand jolted violently in his hand as a massive iron ball materialized in mid-air, almost totally filling the remaining space in the chamber.

"Of course," said Ben, "it could also be an Elven Wand of Monstrous Missile Materialization; they both look quite alike."

The ball hung for an instant then seemed to gain weight and dropped downwards abruptly to smash with almost unimaginable violence on the floor. Cracks crazed the flagstones like a fractured pane of glass and with an earthquake rumble the floor fell in.

Barmy found himself sliding into a funnel. He twisted and scrabbled desperately in a vain attempt to get a grip. For a moment he thought he had managed it, but his fingers tore free. Out of the corner of his eye he saw one of his companions – he thought it might be Ben – disappearing downwards. Somebody yelled and somebody else screamed. Barmy was sliding, the rough edges of crumbling flagstones tearing at his armour. Then, suddenly, he was over an edge and plunging into a pit of darkness.

104

Nineteen

Barmy came to with Eynek's tongue licking his face. He
had a throbbing head and a lump the size of a hen's egg
on his temple, but was otherwise in quite reasonable
shape, considering. He seemed to have been the last to
regain consciousness. Pendragon was pacing with a pro-
nounced limp and Facecrusher had tied her left arm in a
makeshift sling, but the others showed no obvious signs of
injury. In fact Rowan seemed positively cheerful.

"Ger off, Eynek!" Barmy said and forced himself painfully to his feet. His knees buckled and he threw an arm
around the great dog's neck for support. Lauren materialized beside him at once.

"Are you all right, Barney?" she asked.

"Yes, I think so. Just a bit . . ." He let it trail and
asked, "What about you? Are you hurt?"

"No." She giggled quietly. "I fell on the Reverend
Bong."

"Where –?" Barmy began, but the sight before him
stopped him dead, his heart suddenly pounding.

They were still underground, but for a moment he could
hardly believe it. He was standing on a grassy terrace near
the banks of a river which flowed into a vast, ornamental
lake. Beyond the lake towered a fairy-tale palace of delicate towers and spires, nestling among trees which housed
exotic, brightly-coloured birds of every shape and hue. It
might have been a parkland . . . except that it was not.

Barmy blinked, still utterly unable to comprehend what

he was seeing. Of all the oddities he had experienced since the day he first Quasimodo Walked through a Möbius Warp, this was by far the most alien, most unbelievable, most spectacular, most overwhelming. Neither the river nor the lake contained water, but were entirely filled with liquid mercury. The trees beyond seemed to be carved from jade, the birds within them made from silver, gold and other costly metals.

He tore his eyes away and looked up. Overhead, sweeping from horizon to horizon, was a vast dome of brass and copper plates, a patchwork sky, studded here and there with rare crystals and precious stones to represent stars. The landscape – all the landscape – was one huge artefact. Even the grass on which he stood proved, on closer examination, to be composed of individual strands of silk.

There was light here: not the gloomy fungoid glow he had seen in the corridors and chambers they had left, but a cool illumination with a bluish tinge, perhaps a little brighter than full moonlight.

"This isn't possible!" Barmy breathed.

"No, it's not, is it?" remarked the Bong.

"Where are we?" Barmy asked, at last completing the question he had begun an eternity ago.

"Still in the tomb," the Bong said. "Or rather under it – although I have a theory this is the *real* tomb: the pyramid thing up above is just a way of confusing robbers. We fell through the roof," the Bong continued. "Or the floor, depending on how you look at it."

"What happened to that giant ball Ben conjured up?"

"It rolled into the quicksilver lake," Pendragon said. "It must be hundreds of feet deep."

Still dazed, Barmy glanced upwards. He could see no

106

indication of the ball having broken through the vault of the roof.

"It's self-repairing," the Reverend Bong said. "Sealed itself over in minutes. Never saw the like of it before."

"King Tarantulus must have hired somebody who knew a lot about magic, Barmy," Ben put in. He sighed and added, "They don't make it like that any more."

Barmy still could not quite take it all in. "How far does it go on for?" he asked eventually.

"I don't know, Barmy. I've only just got here myself," Ben said.

"We decided we'd better wait until you came round before we started exploring," the Bong said.

"And give my foot time to heal," remarked Pendragon. "I hurt it pretty badly in the fall."

"Is it better now?"

"It is agony, but I can endure it," said Pendragon bravely. He had the irritating habit of always trying to impress.

"Where do we start?" Barmy asked. He addressed the question to the Reverend Bong, who still seemed to be leading the party despite the fact that he'd nearly killed them with the lightning wand.

"The palace," said the Bong with finality. "My theory is that King Tarantulus would have had that built as his actual tomb, with the rest of this –" He waved a hand around airily to denote the whole incredible scene. " – just window dressing. If there's real treasure about, we'll find it in the palace, mark my words."

"What do you think we should do, Facecrusher?" Aspen asked.

"I think we should break up into small two-person groups – Lancie and Ben, Barmy and Lauren, you and

I, Aspen, and Rowan and Eynek. That way we –"

"Here, what about me?" protested Pendragon loudly.

"You can join our group, Draggie," Ben offered.

"No, thanks."

"You go with Rowan and Eynek," Facecrusher said firmly. "If we're split up and anything does happen – a trap sprung, anything like that – it will minimize the damage."

"But you think we should head for the palace, don't you?" Lancelot asked.

"Oh yes – it's the only thing that makes sense."

"How do we get across the lake?" Rowan asked.

"We don't," said the Bong. "We go around it."

Circling the lake took nearly three hours, since every step of the way had to be checked for traps. It was a nervewracking experience, compounded by the fact that they managed to get lost twice. Over and over Barmy had to keep reminding himself that he was still underground and that every plant and shrub he passed was artificial, created from metal, stone, wood, glass, silk or what-have-you and magically preserved to withstand the rigours of the centuries.

Every blade of grass in this whole extensive landscape was a work of art. At one point, as they prodded and poked their way through a delightful little wood of polished soapstone trees, a bird began to sing in the branches, trilling a series of clear high notes as delightfully as any nightingale. It sounded so natural that for a moment Barmy walked on without thinking, then realized how few birds live underground and turned back to find a mechanical creation of ivory and jade, warbling by magic or by clockwork.

"How was that set off?" Facecrusher demanded.

"It's only a clockwork bird," Pendragon said, as his group joined the others.

"Yes," Facecrusher agreed sourly, "and it could have been a clockwork anything . . . or an alchemical bomb." She glared around at everyone. "We have to be far more careful."

Pendragon pouted, as he always did when someone slapped him down.

They finally reached the palace, which was set in a clearing and looked even more impressive close up than it had done at a distance. It was surrounded by a quick silver moat, but this was more ornamental than practical since a massive drawbridge had been lowered.

Across the drawbridge they could see huge open gates of ivory, flanked by magnificently costumed representations of military guards, made from some highly polished metal and armed with crossbows even more ornately carved than the one that Ben habitually carried.

"How does it look?" Facecrusher asked.

Aspen stepped forward and smashed her stone-ball weapon on the ground, then moved forward a few paces before smashing it again. It was a technique they had evolved which was designed to spring any traps ahead, a sort of primitive equivalent of a minesweeper. After a while, Aspen said, "Seems clear."

"Tally-ho!" said Lancelot and started across the drawbridge. Some dark instinct of foreboding seized Barmy's mind and without knowing why, he was about to call out a warning. Facecrusher beat him to it. "No, Lancie!" she screamed. As she did so, one of the costumed guards turned with mechanical precision, raised his crossbow and discharged the bolt.

As had happened once before, Barmy found himself

watching the scene in slow motion. The bolt flew straight and true, piercing the Bong's breastplate as if it were paper and flinging him backwards in a splay of arms and legs to land with a resounding crash on the boardwalk of the drawbridge. His eyes stared sightlessly upwards at the brass dome high above.

Aspen was running towards him. "No!" Barmy screamed in panic as the second mechanical guard raised his weapon and swung it to aim at her. Barmy's paralysis broke and he too began to run forward. The guard fired just as she reached the point where Lancie lay, the fingers of one hand now trailing limply in the silver moat. But unlike the Bong, Aspen was prepared for the attack and dropped into a forward roll so that the bolt flew harmlessly above her head.

Then she was on the mechanical men, flaying them in a fury with the stone-ball weapon she had carried from the first day Barmy saw her. The automata shattered in a protesting whir of metal cogs and levers. Barmy reached the body of the Bong and stopped, not wanting to confirm what he already knew. Ben rushed past him and knelt down, feeling for a pulse. After a moment he looked up, his brown eyes filled with bewilderment.

"Barmy," he said, "Lancie's dead."

Twenty

After a while, Aspen sat down on the floor beside Barmy and slipped her arm around his shoulders. "There was nothing any of us could do," she said quietly. "You know what Lancie was like – always racing ahead and jumping in without thinking. Something like this had to happen some time."

Barmy nodded silently. He felt numb. They had tried to bury Lancie in a glade among jade trees, but the ground there – and everywhere else for that matter – proved impossible to dig; the entire gigantic cavern, it seemed, had been hewn from solid rock.

It was Facecrusher, her features stony as the ground, who suggested laying out the body in a room of the palace until they could find a way to the surface. Then they could return and take it back for burial. Or, alternatively, as Pendragon suggested, they might decide to leave it where it was – they were, after all, in the most elaborate tomb ever created. Aspen and Rowan had gone ahead to check for traps and to choose a room.

Now, inside the building, Barmy was paying his last respects to an old friend.

After a moment, Aspen said, "Come on, Barmy, there's nothing more you can do here."

"There's nothing more any of us can do, Barmy," Ben said at his shoulder. They took his arm and led him gently away. He could feel tears flowing down his cheeks.

They emerged into a short corridor and headed, through

an arch, to the courtyard immediately beyond the draw-bridge. There were the remains of two more mechanical guards flanking the arch, destroyed by Aspen like the first pair when she and Rowan searched for a suitable chamber to lay out Lancie. The courtyard was otherwise featureless and empty.

"All right," Facecrusher said grimly, having taken charge with the practised ease of a natural leader, "we've all had a bad shock and a deep sorrow, but let's do what Lancie would have wanted us to do and learn from it. Every one of us knew the Tomb of Tarantulus had a lethal reputation before we set foot inside it."

She straightened her shoulders in a totally subconscious gesture of determination. "We knew that – we all knew that – and now we know what happens when one of us forgets it. Lancie forgot it just for a second and paid with his life." She paused, staring round them grimly. "But that's the last one of us who's going to get hurt. We are going to treat this place with the respect it deserves. We are going to explore this tomb and we are going to find our way out, all of us, the rest of us, safely and alive! Any questions?"

"Grr," Eynek said.

"He was only cheering," Rowan explained.

"Do you have a plan, Farecrusher?" Ben asked. He had an obsession with plans.

"Of a sort, Ben," Facecrusher said. "First, we stick together. No wandering about to –"

"I thought you said we should break up into groups," Pendragon said aggressively.

"That was *outside*," Facecrusher explained patiently, obviously unaware how odd it sounded to describe the huge subterranean cavern as *outside*. She looked around.

112

"Inside the palace it's better we stick together. It's not just traps – I have a feeling everything in here might not necessarily be dead. So no wandering off to explore on your own. Clear, Rowan?"

"Yes," Rowan said. He managed to look as though he would never dream of wandering off on his own under any circumstances.

"Now, you're under orders," Facecrusher continued, "that means that you do what I tell you, when I tell you. Does anybody have any objection to that?"

"I think it should be majority vote," Pendragon said.

"Oh, do shut up, Draggie!" Aspen muttered, but not quietly enough since he turned on her angrily.

"I won't shut up, Aspen! I have every right to give an opinion. I think it should be majority vote."

"What should be majority vote, Draggie?" Ben asked curiously.

"Everything," Pendragon said. He looked around, shrugged and added, "Any decisions that have to be made."

"There isn't time for that," Aspen began impatiently. "Decisions will have to be taken in an emergency and –"

"Why don't we vote on whether I should be leader?" Facecrusher broke in. Four hands went into the air at once and Eynek wagged his tail.

After a moment, Pendragon slowly raised his hand as well, pouting.

"Seems to be settled," Facecrusher said. "Let's move on!"

"Now?" asked Pendragon.

"Now," said Facecrusher firmly; and walked back through the archway.

The palace proved to be a lot more spooky than it

113

looked from the outside. Like the marvellous landscape, it was contrived as an exact replica: the home of a great king. But where the real home of a great king would have been teeming with courtiers and servants, this subterranean building was populated by figures made of metal or terracotta. They lurked in every corridor and room, cunningly modelled and often painted to appear as lifelike as possible.

Aspen, who had taken the lead in order to bash the corridor floor with her weapon, stopped so suddenly that Pendragon walked into her.

"Why did you do that?" Pendragon asked angrily, nervousness making him more aggressively rude than ever.

"Shut up!" Aspen hissed. "I'm listening."

"What are you listening for, Asprin?"

"Hush, Ben."

"Sorry, Asprin."

Facecrusher joined her. "Up ahead?"

Aspen nodded.

"Think you can trigger it?"

"What are you talking about?" Pendragon asked loudly. "Come on, will somebody tell me?"

"Be quiet, Draggie!"

"One more word . . ." Facecrusher warned.

But Aspen suddenly darted forward to slam her stone-ball weapon against the right-hand wall. The force of her blow was not particularly hard, but there was an immediate *boinnnnng* as a hidden spring snapped and a panel opened to spill a writhing mass of snakes and scorpions on to the corridor floor. Aspen began methodically to crush them. "Thought I heard something," she muttered with obvious satisfaction.

"Strewth!" Pendragon exclaimed, wide-eyed. "We

114

would have been in big trouble if we'd walked into that!"

"Tarantulus must have used magic to preserve the snakes and things. Otherwise they wouldn't have lived all this time," Facecrusher said and shrugged to improve the fit of her breastplate. "Come on, Aspen – just because you did a good job doesn't mean we can hang around here all day."

Aspen grinned and started down the corridor again, spinning her stone weapon as she went.

Through his grief, something was nagging at the back of Barmy's mind and as they reached a silent banquet hall where a frozen terracotta feast was in full swing, it surfaced abruptly.

"Facecrusher . . ."

"Not now, Barmy." She was sweeping the seated figures with her eyes, trying to discover if any was more than it seemed. "What do you reckon, Aspen?"

"I can smash the figures if you like."

"We may not need to," Facecrusher said. "None of them is armed."

"Suppose one of us went in . . ."

"Yes, I will." Before Aspen could protest, Facecrusher stepped into the room. She examined the immediate surroundings minutely, then returned to the door, still watching in case there was any hint of danger.

Barmy waited. When she was satisfied, she said, "Yes, Barmy, what is it?"

"I was wondering if we were paying too much attention to the figures," Barmy said.

Facecrusher blinked. Eventually she said, "They're dangerous. We've seen how dangerous."

Barmy licked his lips thoughtfully. "If you were trying

to set a trap for somebody, Facecrusher, would you show them what it was?"

"No, of course no–" She suddenly saw what he was getting at. "You mean the mechanical figures at the gate are meant to make us suspicious of all the figures inside?"

"Well, the figures at the gate are traps in their own right," said Barmy. "But once they've been sprung – and they would be once anybody stepped on to the drawbridge – it doesn't make much sense to set up any more of the same. Anybody coming in would be bound to be on the lookout for them. But if you filled the place with similar figures –"

"Then everybody would be so busy watching them, they would miss the *real* traps," Lauren said. She frowned. "Why didn't I think of that?"

They moved cautiously into the room.

"What's that smell?" Ben asked suddenly.

"What smell?"

"A cross between rotten eggs and boiled cabbage," Ben said.

"I can't smell anything," Pendragon said, sniffing.

"Grr."

"Eynek can," Rowan said.

"So can I," said Lauren. "It's the first thing I've been able to smell since we arrived here."

"I don't think –" began Pendragon. He stopped, crossed his eyes comically and fell flat on his back.

"Oh, come on, Draggie, don't start clowning no–"

Barmy, who had never thought of Pendragon as the type who was much given to clowning, noticed Lauren's words were fading in and out, as if someone were fiddlng with her volume control. It struck him as quite amusing and he began to grin.

116

"It's gas," Ben said to nobody in particular.

"It's *great* gas!" Barmy agreed, giggling a little.

"You're right, Ben," said Facecrusher grimly. "That's gas all right – *poison* gas! My husband used it at one time; I remember the smell." She swooped on the prostrate Pendragon and hefted him over one shoulder in a single movement. "All right – everybody out!!"

Her tone sobered Barmy, but as he swung towards the door, a thick metal shutter slammed down with appalling violence, sealing it completely.

Twenty-one

"Lauren!" Barmy gasped in alarm, (surprisingly for somebody who always claimed he couldn't stand the sight of his sister). Then, immediately, "Aspen!" He took a breath, imagining he could feel the acrid rasp of the poison gas in his throat and looked around in rising panic. The only way out of this crazy banquet hall with its immobile, painted figures seemed to be the door through which they had entered.

Facecrusher and Ben were both hammering uselessly on the metal shutter. Aspen, who kept a very cool head in a crisis, moved over to the opposite wall, calling, "See if you can find where the gas is coming in and block it!" Lauren and Rowan began systematically to examine the area of skirting where the wall joined the floor.

"It's no good," Facecrusher said. "This isn't going to budge!" For some reason she seemed particularly susceptible to the gas: her face had taken on a distinctly bluish tinge and she was swaying slightly, like someone who had drunk too much mead.

Barmy was fairly certain the fumes were affecting him as well. His thinking seemed to be far more muddled than usual and he found he had to be very careful when he moved. All the same, unless his imagination was running riot, he thought he could just catch a faint hiss from somewhere near the bottom of the long banquet table. He decided to back his own judgement and follow the sound.

"There's something here!" called Rowan. He had momentarily abandoned the skirting to move a small picture hanging on the wall. Behind it was a grille.

As Barmy glanced across, he saw Facecrusher reel so badly that she was forced to support herself with one hand against a pillar.

Aspen joined Rowan, standing on tiptoe to stare into the grille. "It's a duct of some sort," she said, "but I think it's blocked. There's no gas coming out of it anyway."

Facecrusher slid to the floor and spread out in a graceless heap. Her eyes remained open and she was still breathing, but it was obvious she was no longer conscious.

"You keep looking, Aspen, Barmy, Rowan," Ben said. "I'll see to Facecrusher." Of all of them, he seemed the least affected by the gas.

"Grr."

"You keep helping too, Eynek. I didn't mean to overlook you."

The sound was faint but definite and the smell was stronger in this section of the room. Barmy dropped down on his hands and knees and started to crawl under the banquet table. There he stopped, suddenly very chill. There was machinery hidden beneath the table.

Barmy backed out. "Have a look at this, Aspen!" he called.

She joined him almost at once, squatting down to look. "What is it?" she asked, subconsciously dropping her voice in an effort to avoid alarming the others.

"Machinery," Barmy said.

"I can see it's machinery," Aspen said without rancour. "What do you think it does?"

"It's not doing anything at the moment," Barmy said. "There are a couple of dead rats gumming up the works

119

– you can see them if you crawl right under. I thought the gas might be coming in from there."

"And is it?"

"I don't know."

"Do you think the machinery might have something to do with it?"

"I don't think so," Barmy said worriedly. "The gas is coming in, but the machinery isn't working because of the rats."

"What are you two whispering about?" asked Lauren, kneeling down beside them.

"Barmy's found some machinery under the table," Aspen said. "How's Facecrusher?"

"Unconscious," Lauren said. "And Pendragon hasn't moved. We're going to have to do something quickly."

Aspen frowned. "I wonder why they went down so fast? They're both very strong."

"And they're both very tall," Lauren said. "I have a theory this gas is lighter than air, so it will have a tendency to collect near the ceiling and work its way downwards. So the tall ones will be breathing it first. We're still standing and Ben's hardly showing any signs at all."

"Barmy's a bit bigger than we are," Aspen said. "What about him?"

"Only a bit," Lauren said. "Besides, he's been crawling around on his hands and knees."

"I wish you two wouldn't talk about me as if I wasn't here," Barmy said crossly.

"Sorr–" Aspen began.

"Don't be so touchy, Barney!" Lauren snapped. "What are we going to do about turning off that machinery?"

"Oh, it doesn't control the gas – it's gummed up with dead rats."

"Then you'd better ungum it, hadn't you?"

"Why me?" Barmy asked, suddenly furious.

"Because you're the one who's good with dead rats," said Lauren, smugly and untruthfully. "If it wasn't what started the gas, maybe it will stop it," she went on reasonably. "Anyway, we've got nothing to lose. We haven't found where the gas is coming in and we haven't found a way out." She shrugged. "Maybe the machinery will lift the shutter that blocked the doorway. Maybe it will do something else. It doesn't matter: we can't be much worse off, so we might as well do *something*!" She scowled at him fiercely. "Go on, Barney."

"What's that, Lauren? Hello, Asprin," Ben said, appearing beside them. "Facecrusher and Pendragon are as well as can be expected, but unable to move and failing to respond to stimuli."

"Hello, Ben," Aspen said.

"Go on, Barmy, and clear the rats from the machinery," Lauren said.

He crawled quickly under the table. Close up, the machinery was both extensive and impressive, full of old-fashioned belts and cogs and gears the way real machinery should be. He tried to trace the tracking of the pistons in an attempt to discover what the machinery actually did, but got lost in the maze. He shifted his position slightly and started work (with only a small hesitation) on the rat remains.

He had vaguely expected that the little skeletons might be close to crumbling into dust, but in fact they were not. He prised one out fairly easily. The second took far longer since a leg broke off, but he managed it eventually. He held his breath as it came away, waiting for the rumble of machinery, but nothing happened. He backed out awkwardly.

"I've done it," he said, "but nothing's happened."

"Did you kick it, Barmy?" asked Ben.

"No."

"You have to kick it," said Rowan, who had joined them with Eynek. Barmy noticed that the huge dog looked more subdued than usual, probably due to the increasing effects of the gas.

"I'll kick it," Ben said and walked under the table.

"Ben," called Aspen urgently, "maybe that's not such a goo—"

Whap!

With a roar the banquet hall sprang into life. The sound of a harpsichord filled the air with an old-fashioned rhythm and the seated figures suddenly plunged into the motions of eating and drinking. There was even a steady noise which simulated the hum of background conversation, although no actual words were discernible.

Ben walked out from under the table. "I think I got it going, Barmy," he said proudly.

"Look!" Aspen exclaimed. Despite the danger from the gas, she had stood up. A little light-headed, Barmy followed her example. He saw immediately what had excited her. A panel had opened in one wall, leading into a narrow corridor.

Twenty-two

They dragged out Facecrusher and Pendragon with some difficulty since, though they were still breathing, their bodies had become rigid. Once in to the narrow corridor, however, it was easier; and Aspen even found a way to slide the panel back again, sealing them off from the gas-filled banquet room.

"Is there any gas in here, Eynek?" Barmy asked, figuring that of all of them, Eynek must have the keenest sense of smell.

"Grr," said Eynek uncertainly.

"He's not sure," Rowan said, "but he doesn't think so."

"What do we do about Facecrusher and Pendgragon?" Barmy asked.

"Leave them alone for a few minutes," Lauren suggested. "The effects of the gas should wear off very quickly now they're out of it."

But for once she was wrong. After nearly fifteen minutes, both Facecrusher and Pendragon remained as rigid as ever.

"I don't like the look of this," Ben said eventually, voicing a fear that was near the surface of all their minds.

"Neither do I," said Rowan abruptly. "I think it may have been Ankhespander's Death Cap Swamp Gas."

"Grr!" Eynek exclaimed in sudden alarm.

"What's Ankhespander's Death Cap Swamp Gas?" Barmy asked, only marginally less disturbed.

"It's something the Thieves' Guild developed," Rowan

123

said. "It causes total paralysis; the idea being that you administer it in small doses then rob them. Once you give them the antidote, they recover fully inside twenty minutes – plenty of time for you to make your getaway."

"That's great!" Barmy exclaimed. "If it *is* Ankhespander's Death Cap Swamp Gas as you think, all you have to do is –" He caught sight of Rowan's expression. "You haven't got the antidote?"

Rowan shook his head. "Not with me, no. I'd have to go back to the Guild for some . . ."

"What do we do with Facecrusher amd Pendragon in the meantime?" Lauren asked bluntly.

Rowan looked even more uncomfortable. "That's the thing, Lauren – there's nothing you *can* do with them. They'll stay stiff and staring until they get the antidote. There's no other known cure."

Lauren, who was quick on the uptake, said, "Won't they starve?"

Rowan scratched the side of his nose and failed to meet her eye. "Eventually," he said.

"This strikes me as a very good reason for finding a way out of the tomb as quickly as possible," said Aspen calmly.

Lauren nodded. "Yes."

"We have to elect a new leader," Ben said. "I think it should be Aspen because Lauren's so bossy, Rowan's too shifty and Barmy's too dim."

"What about Eynek?" Rowan asked.

"Couldn't we just do without a leader?" suggested Aspen. "There aren't very many of us left and we're more or less agreed on what we should be doing." She looked around. "Aren't we?"

Barmy started to nod, but Rowan said, "I think we should loot the tomb. We'll never get a chance like this again."

"If we loot the tomb, Facecrusher and Pendragon may die."

"I suppose you're right," Rowan said. "But I want you to know it goes against my principles."

"All right," Aspen said, "so we try to find a way out as quickly as possible." She hesitated. "What are we going to do with Facecrusher and Pendragon? We can't very well carry them with us in that state, but I'm a bit worried about leaving them here."

"What do you think, Rowan?" Lauren asked.

Rowan glanced around. "This place will be as safe as any," he said at last.

"And as dangerous," Ben remarked.

"Yes, all right, and as dangerous. But it would be just as dangerous to take them with us, even if we could–"

"All right," said Aspen, who seemed to have assumed the role of leader whether she wanted it or not. "Let's not discuss this any more. Let's make them as comfortable as we can and as safe as we can, then let's search for a way out as quickly as possible. Once we find one, we'll either come back for them, or make a run for the Keep to get the antidote, depending . . ."

"Depending on what, Asprin?"

"How should I know, Ben? Just depending!" Aspen snapped. The strain of their situation was obviously getting to her. She *never* got angry with Ben.

Making Facecrusher and Pendragon comfortable was far from easy. Their paralysis was absolute, but they seemed to be elastic. Ben and Barmy forced Pendragon into a sitting position easily enough, but when they let him go, he sprang upright at once and regained his original stance. They were no more successful with Facecrusher. Eventually they propped them both against a wall and left them. It seemed callous, but there was nothing else to do.

The narrow corridor ran due north for almost fifty yards unbroken by doors or branches, then turned west at right angles. They moved forward with, if anything, even more caution than they had shown before, examining every bit of the floor and walls before they took each step. But despite it all, they missed something. As the last of the reduced party turned the corner, a second metal shutter slammed down, trapping them within the new section.

"Oooow!" exclaimed Eynek, who had been bringing up the rear.

Barmy swung round, but Rowan beat him to it. "It's all right," Rowan said. "It just nipped the end of his tail. No damage done – he's a dreadful baby."

"Grr," Eynek protested savagely.

Aspen, Lauren and Ben began to examine the shutter, then the surrounding wall in the hope of finding a control mechanism. It quickly became evident there was no way of getting back. They looked at one another. "Pendragon," Lauren said softly.

"And Facecrusher," Aspen said.

There was a moment's silence as the implications of their situation sank in fully. If they could not get back, even finding a way out would make no difference to Facecrusher and Pendragon; they would die of thirst, trapped within this silent subterranean palace. It occurred to Barmy that the rumours and the legends gave totally the wrong impression. The Tomb of Tarantulus did not just *contain* traps – the place itself was one huge trap.

The more he thought about it, the more it made sense. The honeycomb cube of magical artefacts (openly displayed and entirely unprotected) would surely attract intruders like a magnet. If they didn't manage to kill themselves by fiddling with the magical toys, they would certainly precipitate themselves – as the party had actually done – into the vast, landscaped cavern.

Once there, of course, it was the palace that would attract them like a magnet. And the whole thing had been planned so that anyone entering the palace was on a strictly one-way trip to join the long-dead king.

He opened his mouth to share these insights, but shut it again as a low, ominous rumbling sound reached his ears. At first he could not place what it might be.

"Oh good grief!" Aspen exclaimed.

Barmy turned to follow the direction of her gaze and his eyes widened in horror. Rolling slowly down the corridor was a huge stone ball of a size more than ample to crush every one of them as flat as pancakes.

Twenty-three

"Above it!" Aspen screamed.

Barmy looked up, but could see nothing of any interest above the rolling ball.

Aspen caught him by the shoulder and actually shook him. "Climb!" she shouted in his ear.

He might have remained there indefinitely, wondering what was going on, if Lauren had not suddenly realized what Aspen was getting at. "Like this!" Lauren called. "There's room above it!" She braced her feet against one wall of the narrow corridor, her back against the other and began to inch her way upwards.

Barmy groaned inwardly. He was useless at this sort of thing. All the same, he had no choice now. He turned sideways, leaned back against the wall, then gave a little hop and tried running upwards. Incredibly it worked; at least he found himself fairly securely jammed between the two walls. He glanced towards the approaching ball and began to edge his way upwards.

It was even more difficult than he expected. The great ball was rolling slowly, but very surely. With nothing better to do, he watched it in horrified fascination as he inched upwards. As it came closer, he was taken by its curiously mottled appearance: it was cratered like a miniature moon.

"Quickly!" Aspen shouted. She seemed to be far more skilled than any of them at this sort of caper, for she was already flattened near the ceiling, with not a hint of a tremble in her leg muscles as she wedged herself in place and waited – hopefully – for the huge ball to roll beneath her.

Barmy glanced around. Even Lauren, who was more intellectual than athletic (and shorter than him) was making better progress. She caught his eye and smiled encouragingly. Barmy redoubled his efforts, hoping to make up in enthusiasm what he lacked in technique. It worked and he was already more than half way up the wall when he noticed Ben.

If Barmy was having difficulty, Ben was in real trouble. The simple fact of the matter was that he was far too short to negotiate the climb as the others did. With the help of one or two small footholds he had managed to climb a little way off the ground, but he could make no further progress. He hung on bravely, the trembling of his muscles changing to a noticeable shake. Suddenly his posture broke and he fell to the floor. It was a short fall, of course, one which would do him no damage at all, but with the ball rolling inexorably onwards, it was a fall which would – almost certainly – cost him his life.

"Aspen!" Barmy screamed. Without thought he abandoned his own attempts to climb and dropped down beside Ben, who had rolled over and was sitting up now, rubbing his nose.

"Hello, Barmy," he said. "I fell down."

"Aspen!" Barmy screamed again. He grabbed Ben's arm and jerked him to his feet. "Come on, idiot," he said. "You should have told us you were in trouble!" He pulled him a few paces up the corridor until he was almost directly underneath Aspen.

"Do you want me to come down?" Lauren called, obviously having realized what he was trying to do.

129

"Stay up!" said Barmy. "But get closer to Aspen. Can you?"

"Yes, I think so." She began to edge over.

Barmy could not understand why the gigantic ball had not crushed them at this time, but it was panic affecting his judgement. When he looked, it was still rolling, still terrifyingly close, but still far enough away for him to do what he had to do. The big question was, was it far enough away for him to do what he had to do and then climb to safety himself?

He pushed this question hurriedly out of his mind, bent and locked his fingers together so his hands made a cradle. "Come on, Ben – up you go!"

"What do you want me to do, Barmy?"

"Stand on my hands and reach up towards Aspen and Lauren," Barmy said. "I'll give you a boost if you still can't reach."

"What about you, Barmy?" He glanced towards the rolling ball, now dangerously close.

"Ben, we haven't time to discuss this!" Barmy screamed, his panic suddenly surfacing.

"All right, Barmy," Ben said meekly. He stepped nimbly into the cradle of Barmy's hands.

Barmy tried to straighten and felt a stab of pain in his lumbar region. The plan was sound, but he was just not strong enough to carry it out. Ben teetered a little.

"He's too heavy!" Barmy screamed in despair.

Then Rowan was beside him. "Again," Rowan said. "I'll push." He gripped Ben around the waist.

With a massive effort Barmy straightened. "Two, six – heave!" Rowan grunted. Ben bounced upwards. Lauren reached for his outstretched hands and missed, but Aspen had a truer eye and caught one wrist. "I've got him!" She

130

jerked with surprising strength and Ben sailed upwards. Lauren had his free hand now and suddenly he was dangling between them near the ceiling.

"Move, Barmy!" Aspen commanded.

"Rowan . . .?"

"Go!" urged Rowan.

Abandoning all thought of style, Barmy braced his back against the wall and started to work himself upwards in a sweat of urgency. He was not, he thought, going to make it. The rolling ball was too close, the ceiling too far. He slipped, dropping down nearly two feet before he could stop himself and his suspicion was confirmed. But he kept climbing, since there was nothing else he could do.

Lauren was shouting something, but he could not make out the words over the rumbling of the massive ball. It was only seconds away from him and he knew for certain now it would strike him. When it did, he would fall and the ball would crush him to a pulp. In all probability, there would be little pain, but the mess would be awful.

He watched Ben draw up his legs then he, Lauren and Aspen vanished safely behind the rolling ball, with Aspen shouting something to him. He wondered what they were trying to tell him. The ball rumbled inexorably onwards, reached him –

– and, incredibly, passed under him! Barmy remained braced against the walls, astounded. He had felt the rough surface scrape his back, but by some miracle, it had not dislodged him. The ball crashed with appalling force against the shutter which had trapped them in this section of corridor.

He hung, braced, shivering and trembling with reaction. If the others were saying anything to him, he did not hear them. Some part of his mind was gibbering about the

131

futility of it all, although he could not understand what it was talking about. He was safe! They were safe!

The shivering died down slowly and his head cleared a little. Out of the corner of his eye, he could see Aspen and Lauren still braced like himself near the ceiling, although they seemed to have let Ben drop. To his surprise, he noticed that Aspen seemed to be weeping, although he could not imagine why. They were safe. They were all safe. They had survived –

Futility!

– the rolling ball and now they were –

Now they were trapped! Still trapped! Always trapped! There were no doors leading off the corridor and now that the rolling ball had passed, he could see it ended in a blank stone wall.

Twenty-four

"This corridor's a dead end," Ben's voice floated up to him. "Isn't there always something, Rowan? Rowan . . .?"

Suddenly Barmy's eyes lighted on a crack in the ceiling. A *regular* crack, describing a perfect square. He saw Lauren and Aspen begin to edge their way down. "I think I've found a trapdoor," he said. He shifted his position slightly, braced himself more firmly, reached out with one hand and pushed. It didn't open, but he thought he felt it give a little. "It's a trapdoor in the ceiling. We aren't really trapped." Although maybe they were. He pushed again and still the trapdoor did not open. "Listen," he said, "can somebody give me a hand here?" The trapdoor opened suddenly. "It's okay, it's okay – I've got it!"

He was looking up into a narrow, unlighted shaft with, to his delight, the end of a metal ladder just visible about a foot or so inside. "I think I've found a ladder. I'm going to try climbing," he called back, manoeuvring into the shaft. "I'll tell you if it's okay to follow me."

"Barmy!" Aspen called.

But Barmy was already shifting his position, edging over to get a two-handed grip on the ladder. He took a deep breath and relaxed the muscles of his legs. He fell, then swung like a pendulum, rather enjoying the sensation despite the sudden pain in his arms. Then, before he could tire, he pulled himself upwards and swarmed like a monkey into the shaft.

"Barmy!" Aspen called again.

He had no room at all to manoeuvre – the shaft was substantially narrower than the trapdoor – but the ladder felt firm as a rock and seemed to go directly upwards. He started cautiously to climb.

"Are you all right, Barney?" Lauren's voice drifted up from below.

"Yes. It's a bit of a tight fit, but apart from that . . ."

"Listen, Barney," Lauren was calling, but he paid her no attention.

The rungs ended, and Barmy's hands touched what was, perhaps, a wooden ceiling. He fumbled carefully, concentrating hard, trying to sense the outlines of yet another trapdoor, then thought *what the heck* and pushed. The trapdoor opened as easily as if it had been just installed and oiled. Barmy pushed his head through, but found to his chagrin that he could see nothing.

It was not, however, total darkness and as his eyes adjusted, he could see the dim outlines of a chamber full of clutter, like the attic of a lived-in home.

". . . Barmy?"

Lauren's voice again, although he had no idea what she had said. "I'm all right," he called down again. "There's a sort of room up here. I'm going in."

"No, Barmy, don't do –"

But he was already climbing through. He sat with his legs dangling through the opening and looked around, wishing he had some sort of lamp or torch. There was no way he could judge the size of the chamber, but it smelt of must and the looming shapes around him confirmed the impression of a junk room.

"There's lots of stuff here," he called.

"Barney, I really think you should –"

He picked up something and by holding it in front of his nose discovered it was a little, ancient oil lamp. Some reflex made him shake it, but after all this time it was, of course, dry of oil – besides which, he had nothing to light it with. In a moment of whimsy, he rubbed the side.

There was no djinni, but the lamp lit with an audible *pop*! The small, yellow flame burned absolutely steadily, shedding a soft, warm light. Another magical artefact, by the looks of it; and one very useful in his present circumstances.

"Hey," he shouted down, "I've found a magic lamp."

"Don't rub it!" Lauren screamed.

"Not that sort of lamp," said Barmy, grinning. "It just gives light." He held it high and looked around. "I'm in some sort of . . ." His words died, overtaken by amazement.

He was in some sort of treasure chamber. There was absolutely no doubt about it. The dark shapes around him resolved themselves into heaps of jewels and gold coins, statuettes of ivory and jade, bibelots, settings of precious metals, bolts of silk and cloth-of-gold, ingots, crystal goblets, gem-encrusted weaponry for ceremonial use. He saw a ruby large as a pigeon's egg, an emerald even larger.

"Barney . . .? Lauren sounded anxious.

Barmy felt the breath lock in his chest. The wealth collected in this one room was almost unimaginable. He felt his early reservations about looting the tomb collapse in ruins. One gem, just one gem –

"Barney . . .?" Something close to panic now.

– would be enough to buy his parents a car each and keep him in toffee apples for a year. Just one . . .

"I'm all right, Lauren!" he called impatiently. "There's lots of stuff up here."

"What do you mean, Barmy?"

"Gold and stuff, Ben," said Barmy. They had to loot this chamber. To leave it alone would be a downright *sin*!

"What sort of gold and stuff, Barmy?"

"It's the most fantastic treasure you've ever seen! Are you listening, Rowan?"

But before Rowan could answer, Lauren was shouting again, with Aspen calling up at the same time so that he could make out neither of them.

He decided to ignore them and walked forward in the pool of lamplight, heart pounding, eyes glistening with greed. The chamber was far larger than he had imagined at first – in fact, as he moved, he still could see no indication of a wall. And every inch of space was jam-packed with wealth beyond the dreams of avarice. Silver, gold, platinum, ingots and coins . . . a half spilled pouch of perhaps a hundred glistening diamonds . . . artworks of every description . . . even a mind-numbing chariot and pair, life size and cast, so far as he could judge, in solid gold. This was the reality behind the legend of Tarantulus, the ancient king reputed to have been the richest man on earth.

"We're rich!!" Barmy screamed suddenly.

"Barmy . . .?" Aspen's voice this time; and a lot nearer than Lauren's had been.

"Rich!" Barmy screamed again. "Each of us! All of us! There's more money here than we could spend in our whole lives! We could eat off gold plates! We could have diamond bath-taps. We could have a whole fleet of Rolls-Royces each!" She wouldn't know what he meant by a fleet of Rolls-Royces, but he was too excited to care. "This is it!" he shouted. "This is the big one!"

"Barney, calm down!" Lauren called severely.

"Calm down? Calm down? There's enough gold here to *bury* you! There are rubies as big as your head!" A slight exaggeration, but what did he care? Was this how it felt to be a millionaire? "There's millions here. Billions! We can have anything. Anything we want!" He felt lightheaded; all the blood in his body had turned to fizzy lemonade. "Lauren, Aspen – there are solid gold *horses* up here!" He began to giggle, uncontrollably.

He was still giggling when the Guardian of the Treasure skeetered into the circle of his lamplight, eyes glittering like diamonds.

And just as hard.

Twenty-five

It was an enormous golden spider about the size of a St Bernard dog, legs, head and body covered in fine, light fur. It moved, when it moved, with frightening speed. But for the moment it was still, watching him.

Barmy took a backwards step and drew his sword. He was nervous, but not totally terrified. In short, while he was never one to welcome a fight, he quite fancied his chances in this one.

Unless, of course, the creature was not alone.

Barmy looked around, mentally cursing the fact that he had only one small magic lantern to provide his light. The steady flame illuminated a surprisingly large area, but illuminated it at a muted level, softening outlines and casting shadows. The glint of gold was everywhere and it struck him suddenly that the spider itself was exactly the colour of the precious metal which made up so much of the treasure store. It – and a hundred others like it – could have squatted on a heap of gold and remained practically invisible.

Were there others? He strained his eyes, but could see none. The problem was, of course, that before this brute moved, he had seen nothing of it either.

"Barney, what's going on up there?"

He decided he might be better not to answer. For the moment the spider remained immobile and he wanted to do nothing which might prompt it to attack. Instead, he began to back, ever so slowly, ever so cautiously, towards the open trapdoor and its exit shaft. His eyes were locked on those of the golden spider, watching for the slightest indication that it was about to move again.

A second golden spider, smaller than the first (but still large as a cocker spaniel) skeetered out of the gloom to his right and nipped him in the leg above the ankle. The ant armour, which extended to his feet, took most of the force from the bite so that little damage was done, although he felt enough pain to convince him that the skin might be broken. He swung his sword at once, but the creature was no longer there, having retreated into the gloom as swiftly as it had emerged.

It was time, Barmy thought, to risk moving a little faster himself. If the smaller spider could get close, bite through his armour and retreat again without a scratch, he did not care to think what the larger one could do. Besides, the appearance of the second spider had answered one question absolutely: Tarantulus had not contented himself with leaving a single guardian. Barmy suspected the treasure room was crawling with golden spiders, each one ready to defend the treasure with its life. He half turned to make a break for the ladder in the shaft –

– and discovered to his great alarm that his legs would no longer move.

The focus of the problem seemed to be his right leg, just above the ankle, where the spider had bitten him, but the effect had spread to both legs.

And was, he thought, still spreading.

With a gargantuan effort he shifted his left foot a matter of perhaps three inches, then watched with interest as it flopped and rooted itself to the spot. He could feel the paralysis spreading upwards through his body now; and with it a curious lethargy, a curious calm.

He was, he supposed, suffering from the effects of spider venom and would more than likely keel over dead once the poison reached his heart or brain. But he could not find it in himself to panic . . . or even really care. He was warm, he was comfortable, he was relaxed. He had had a good life, if a little short. He had enjoyed the sort of adventures few people ever got a chance to experience. He had made great friends, seen great sights. Why should he worry unduly about a small thing like dying?

Barmy blinked benignly. The world, he thought, was certainly a wonderful place. A wonderful . . . peaceful . . . place. He frowned, bewildered by the fact that he had not realized this before. From a certain viewpoint, he might even consider this lovely spider a friend. From a certain . . . viewpoint . . .

"Barmy, what are you –"

Aspen's head emerged through the opening.

"– doing?" Then, sadly he thought, she began, "Rowan and –" She stopped short, her eyes locked on the giant spider. "Oh, good grief!"

Barmy sighed. "Isn't she the most beautiful thing you have ever seen, Aspen?" he asked. He was glad Aspen had come up, since it gave her an opportunity to see this lovely spider. He wished the others would come up as well. He wished *all* his friends could see this gorgeous creature.

But Aspen was vaulting into the chamber to hurl herself at the golden spider, the great stone weapon ready in her hand.

"No, don't!" Barmy protested weakly. "Don't hit –"

But it was at once too late and unnecessary. As Aspen swung her weapon the spider jumped to one side with blinding speed, so that the stone ball crashed down upon a smallish heap of silver coins, causing them to explode across the chamber like shrapnel. One struck Barmy on the forehead, but did not hurt.

"Lauren! Ben!" Aspen screamed. "Trouble! Get up here! And something's got at Barmy – he's behaving like an idiot!"

"He's *always* behaved that way," said Lauren's voice from the corridor below; but all the same he heard a scrambling as she attempted – he assumed – to reach the ladder.

His hearing seemed to be growing more acute – an interesting phenomenon, Barmy thought. And, of course, he forgave both Aspen and Lauren for suggesting he behaved like an idiot. He especially forgave Lauren who was, after all, his sister whom he loved a great deal. He loved so many other people. Ben and Lancie – poor, dead Lancie – and Facecrusher and Pendragon and Rowan and Eynek and all his friends and all the people in the Keep and his parents and his friends at school and Mrs Fogarty and –

He hesitated. Did he *really* love daft Mrs Fogarty, who would poke the end of her brolly into your stomach quick as look at you? He decided he did. Despite everything. If he could love Pendragon, he could certainly love daft Mrs –

Someone else was scrambling up into the chamber. "Hello, Lauren," Barmy said dreamily. "Come and see the lovely spiders."

"It's not Lauren, Barmy," Ben said. "It's Ben." Two spiders the size of spaniels skeetered out of the gloom on either side of Ben, whose arm moved with blinding speed as he cut each one in half with his short sword. Barmy noticed they bled golden blood. "Did something bite you?" Ben asked.

141

"Mmmm," Barmy said contentedly.

As Ben moved into the chamber, Lauren's head popped out of the trapdoor behind him. To Barmy's surprise, she too was carrying a sword, which was unusual since she tended to avoid physical combat.

"Watch out for spiders, Lauren," Ben said. Then, as an afterthought, he added, "Big ones."

There was little need for the warning, for the beautiful golden spiders were all emerging from hiding now. To Barmy's joy, there were dozens of them, all varying in size. Aspen launched herself upon them, her stone-ball weapon spinning on its chain and humming like a swarm of bees.

"Oh, don't!" Barmy pleaded. "Don't, Aspen – they're so –"

"Your brother appears to be suffering from an obscure biochemical reaction, Lauren, which seems to have affected his psychological processes," Ben explained.

"You mean a spider bite has sent him nuts?" asked Lauren.

"Yes."

"– so lovely," Barmy finished, although no one was listening.

He watched with interest as his sister and his friends attacked the spiders, although he knew there was no need for violence of any sort, just as he knew their violence was pointless since the beautiful spiders were bound to win. . .

. . . as win they did in the fullness of time, while Barmy stood, deliciously warm, deliciously content, sometimes watching the action, but more often lost in his own thoughts.

He emerged from his reverie to find Aspen, Ben and Lauren quite immobile, clear indication that they had –

perhaps through golden spider bites – achieved the same bliss as himself. He smiled. "Isn't this delightful?" he asked no one in particular.

Aspen's jaw jutted and she said nothing, but Ben's eyes were soft and glazed as he breathed, "Yes, Barmy, it's lovely!"

A small army of the giant spiders crawled towards them with an air of great deliberation. They looked, Barmy thought, like the grains of sand on a golden beach stretching to infinity beside a peaceful sea.

Twenty-six

Barmy came to his senses in a vast, colonnaded, marble chamber without very much idea of how he had arrived there.

His arms were free, but his legs were bound with some sort of strong, slender, sticky cable which he guessed must be spider silk. Whatever it was, it was immensely strong for it held his legs absolutely immobile. He noticed that both his sword and the marvellous ant armour had been removed, although the rest of his meagre possessions remained with him.

He was in a throne room. Strange though it seemed, there was no doubt at all about it. The main colonnade of marble pillars – each one shot through with what looked like solid gold – led to rank upon rank of golden spiders, drawn up like soldiers, absolutely immobile, but with glittering gemstone eyes fixed on him. And beyond them, a vast throne, ornately carved from a single block of crystal – quartz, perhaps (although it looked too pure for quartz) because a block that size could not possibly be a diamond.

Could it?

There was a figure on the throne, grandly dressed in cloth of gold, a sceptre in one hand, an orb in the other, both set with precious metals and studded with precious stones in a variety that defied description. On the figure's head was a tall crown, finely wrought in golden filigree.

This was a king, of course, but a dead king. He was

in the presence of the corpse of Tarantulus himself.

"This is very creepy, Barmy," said a familiar voice at his back.

He craned round to find Ben, Aspen and Lauren similarly bound a little way behind him. Aspen seemed unconscious, Lauren dazed, but Ben looked as *compos mentis* as he ever was.

"Don't try to untie yourself, Barmy," Ben advised. "Somebody rotten has put superglue on the ropes."

"Thanks, Ben," Barmy said. He wondered what on earth he was going to do now. And, perhaps more importantly, what the spiders were going to do now.

He turned his gaze back to the throne. Flanking it on either side were two open caskets and a variety of giant urns. Beyond them stood a rank of terracotta bowmen, similar in design to the automaton which had killed the Reverend Bong. Then came a translucent curtain, shimmering with multicoloured hues, beyond which he could just make out the figures of a busy court, presumably more automata like those of the banquet hall. There was no sound. Nothing moved.

"I don't suppose you have a plan?" asked Ben soberly.

"Not as such," said Barmy. "There's not much we can do until we get our feet free; and there's not much hope of that with the spiders watching us."

Aspen groaned suddenly and stretched, then looked around her, dazed.

"Don't try to untie your feet, Asprin," Ben warned. "Somebody rotten has put superglue on the ropes."

"Where are we?" Aspen asked.

"My guess is the burial chamber of King Tarantulus," Barmy said. "It's been done up to look like his throne room."

"How did we get here?"

"I suppose the spiders must have brought us."

"Are you all right, Barmy?"

"Oh yes, fine."

"You were acting a bit oddly," Aspen said warily.

"One of the spiders bit me," Barmy said. "It made me feel funny."

"Do you have a plan, Asprin?" Ben asked.

"Give me a chance, Ben – I've only just woken up."

A thought struck Barmy. "They don't seem to have caught Rowan or Eynek. There's still a chance for us while they're on the loose." He caught sight of Aspen's expression. "What's the matter, Aspen?"

"Didn't you hear me?"

"Hear you?" He felt a sudden panic flowering in his stomach.

Aspen took a deep breath, but suppressed the sight. "I called and called after you and so did Lauren, but I thought you couldn't have heard us. When we were trying to escape from the stone ball . . ." She hesitated, closing her eyes briefly, then went on. "When we were trying to escape, Eynek couldn't climb the wall." She looked around her, seeing nothing. "How could he climb the wall? He was a *dog*, for heaven's sake!"

Was? She said *was*. Realization fell on Barmy like an avalanche. "Eynek's – Enyek's –"

Aspen nodded. She closed her eyes again, biting hard on her bottom lip.

"What about Rowan?" Barmy whispered.

"Rowan stayed with him, Barmy," Ben said gently. "He wouldn't leave Eynek."

Quite suddenly, nothing was important. Barmy felt wave upon wave of sorrow and despair wash over him.

146

Lancie dead. Rowan dead. Eynek dead. And Facecrusher and Pendragon trapped, as good as dead. Only Lauren, Aspen, Ben and himself remaining. He found himself weeping openly, tears streaming down his face.

The sight seemed to pull Lauren together for she said, "Come on, Barney, there's nothing you can do."

"And we need to keep our wits about us, Barmy, otherwise we won't get out of here," Ben said.

"What's the point?" Barmy asked, feeling sorry for himself. "What's the point of anything now?"

"Oh pull yourself together!" Lauren snapped, her tolerance of the maudlin lower than ever. "There's nothing we can do for Rowan and Eynek, but Facecrusher and Pendragon should still be alive. We have to think of them. If we don't get out of this mess we've –"

There was sudden movement among the spiders.

"Trouble," Aspen predicted grimly.

Half a dozen of the creatures detached themselves from the immobile ranks and skeetered forward.

"Do you think they eat people, Barmy?" Ben asked.

But Barmy was too busy to answer him. He was searching through the pockets of his jerkin for something – anything – he might be able to use as a weapon.

One spider reached them and scrabbled at Lauren with one hairy leg. "Yuck!" Lauren exclaimed, pulling away.

"Your arms are still free," Aspen hissed. "See if you can strangle the brute!"

There was nothing. Nothing at all. Not so much as a penknife. The only things he could find were a piece of coloured chalk, a low denomination coin, a grey wad of chewing gum covered in fluff and a –

"Strangle it? Are you out of your –"

"Asprin's right, Lauren," Ben said. "You have to –"

147

A second spider reached them and began to prod at Aspen. She reached for the area of its articulated body that might have been a throat, but it leaped nimbly aside.

"What do they *want*?" Lauren asked, a mixture of anger and rising panic in her voice. "What do they –"

– a little flute of some description. He stared at it, frowning, as a third spider began to prod at him, gently enough, but insistently. Not a flute – a whistle! It was the telepathic ant whistle the Benign Immortal had –

"They *want* something!" Aspen exclaimed. "Get off, you brute!"

"That's what I've just been *telling* –"

There was a thin wail, at the edge of audibility and one of the six spiders skeetered off with a curious rolling gait.

"I bit it in the leg," Ben grinned.

Lauren rolled her eyes, looking as though she might be sick.

There was no chance it would do them any good, of course. Even if it still worked, the ant colony was hundreds of miles away, across a stretch of water. How far away could you hear a telepathic whistle? Not that far, he was sure. And if you *did* somehow hear a telepathic whistle at that distance, how long would it take you to reach the tomb? A week? Two weeks? A month? And even if you somehow managed to reach the tomb while Barmy, Aspen, Ben and Lauren were still alive, what help could you be to them? You were, after all, a tiny little ant – well, a *colony* of tiny little ants – and these were giant spiders, monsters big as dogs, a few as big as ponies. It made no sense at all to blow the whistle.

Barmy blew the whistle.

148

Twenty-seven

A new spider detached itself from the ranks to replace the one Ben had bitten. The six began to circle Aspen, Lauren, Ben and Barmy like Indians round a wagon train.

"What were you blowing just now, Barmy?" Ben asked curiously.

"It's just a telepathic ant whistle," Barmy said, "but it won't work at this dista–" He stopped in mid sentence, galvanized.

What can we do for you, Barmy Jeffers, friend of the Benign Immortal?

"It won't work at this what, Barmy?" Ben asked. "And why are you looking at me all funny?"

It was the modulated soprano of the ant queen speaking in his head!

Not the queen - the colony. That has been explained to you.

Sorry, Barmy thought. *Sorry*. Then, more to the point, *Where are you?*

"Barmy, why won't you answer me?"

Nearby.

But you can't be nearby! Barmy protested. *How can you be nearby? You're hundreds of miles away and I've only just blown the whistle!*

We are not the same colony you visited, Barmy Jeffers. That colony was one of our sisters, living on the mainland.

You mean any *colony can hear the whistle?*

Of course.

149

And you'll help us? How was another matter.

"Asprin, I think Barmy's had a relapse from spider poison."

Aspen leaned forward. "He does look a bit odd, Lauren . . ."

Any friend of a friend of the Benign Immortal is a friend of ours, the colony said obscurely.

"Maybe –"

"I'm all right, I'm all right!" Barmy said impatiently. "I'm just talking to some ants."

"He *has* had a relapse," Lauren frowned.

"Just leave me alone, will you?" Barmy snapped. Mentally he said, *Exactly where are you?"*

Look to your right.

Barmy looked to his right. A thin black column of soldier ants was marching across the floor.

"There *are* ants here, Lauren," Ben said. "Are those the ones you're talking to, Barmy?" A golden spider rushed in to tug at him and he bit that one in the leg as well.

"Yes," Barmy said. He'd heard some hairy stories about soldier ants, but could they really take on giant spiders?

We can take on anything, said the voice inside his head, *but why do you need our help against these spiders?*

"Why?" echoed Barmy. "Why? Are you out of your mind? They're going to eat us!"

"Who is, Barmy?" Ben asked curiously. To Lauren he said, "I think he's worried about the spiders."

"Sorry," Barmy said, realizing he had spoken aloud.

They're not going to eat you – they want your help.

Our help? To Ben he said, "They're not going to eat us!"

"You just try to relax, Barney," Lauren said soothingly. "Everything's going to be all right."

They've been waiting for years for human beings to

find the tomb, the ant voice said inside his head.

How do you know this? Barmy demanded.

The marching column of soldier ants formed a ring around them. The spiders stopped circling and retreated to a distance of about two metres, then froze into that familiar immobility.

They told us.

"You can *talk* to the spiders?" Barmy asked them incredulously.

"No, of course not," Aspen said.

"I think he's hearing voices," Lauren murmured. "We had a cousin who went that way once – maybe it's in the family."

Telepathically.

How come I can't hear them?

You're not an ant.

I can hear you!

That's different. It's a question of wavelength. As a human, you're close enough to the ant wavelength to communicate with us. Spiders are further out – we can only just hear them ourselves.

"Those ants are guarding us," Ben remarked. "I've never seen ants do that before."

All right, Barmy said, *all right. Why have they been waiting for humans and how can we help them?*

By resurrecting King Tarantulus, the ant voice said.

"What?" Barmy screamed.

"Nobody said anything, Barmy," Ben assured him.

That's what they've been waiting for.

This is crazy! Crazy! A breakaway column of ants had swarmed on to his legs and, apparently unaffected by the superglue, was eating away his bonds, but Barmy scarcely noticed. *They're mad! We're surrounded by loony tunes spiders*! He felt as if his head was going to burst. "How do they expect me to resurrect King Tarantulus!!!!????"

"Maybe you could use this," said a familiar voice behind him.

Barmy swung round and jumped to his feet. The spider silk snapped, showering ants in all directions. "Sorry," Barmy muttered, then, more sensibly, *Sorry*. He stared, eyes wide, jaw slack. Eventually he said, "Rowan!" Then a moment later, "Eynek!"

"Right!" said Rowan. He was straddling Eynek's back and waving an emerald tablet. Neither of them looked any flatter than usual.

"I –" Barmy stuttered. "We –"

"We thought you were dead, Rowan," Ben said.

"Grr."

"Eynek says he doesn't think so."

"That's good, Rowan," Ben said calmly. "Barmy, if you can really talk to the ants, would you tell them to eat my legs free too?"

"Don't touch the spiders, Eynek," Barmy said hurriedly. "You neither, Rowan – or any of you. They just want our help." He blinked. "In resurrecting King Tarantulus!"

"This is insane!" Lauren said.

"It's not!" Barmy said, although privately he had his doubts. "They think we can do it. They've been *waiting* for us because they think we can –"

The spiders say King Tarantulus did not die when everybody thought he did. He decided to become an Immortal instead and had this vast secret cavern built to live in with his spiders.

"He *lived* here?" Barmy asked, apparently interrupting himself.

"Who did?" Ben asked, confused.

For many thousands of years. Then he became careless and neglected part of the Immortality Process and so died. But his spiders lived on, waiting for somebody who could resurrect him.

It made sense of a sort. At least Barmy knew Immortals weren't impossible, having met one in an ant hill. If Tarantulus had simply disappeared, living in this palace in the secret cavern, people would have assumed him dead. With his spiders to look after him and his Immortality Process – whatever that was – to keep him healthy, he might well have lasted a long time. In fact, now that Barmy came to think of it, the Benign Immortal of the Saffron Robe claimed to have lived in Tarantulus' day, so there was no reason to believe Tarantulus himself could not have survived if he had the secret of immortality. Except that he seemed to have screwed it up somewhere along the line, for the thing on the throne was a corpse if ever Barmy had seen one.

And now his spiders wanted him brought back to life! "How are we supposed to resurrect him?" Barmy screamed.

"I told you," Rowan said. "You can use this." He slid down from Eynek's back and casually tossed the emerald tablet towards Barmy.

Something about the colour rang bells in Barmy's head. He glanced at the inscribed writing, so ancient he had difficulty reading it, but it was definitely a formula for turning lead to gold in the alchemical tradition. So he had the tablet he had promised to bring back to the Benign Immortal. Which would have been great news under normal circumstances, but was useless now. He looked up at Rowan. "This is no good for resurrection."

"The other side," said Rowan.

153

"Didn't think of that," said Barmy sheepishly. He turned the tablet over. Cut into the back were full instructions for a resurrection spell. He read through them quickly, but carefully, trying to remember everything the Amazing Presto taught him. It was unfamiliar stuff, but the *style* seemed genuine enough, in that it followed the basic principles of magic as he understood them. He looked up at Rowan. "Do you think this will really work?" he asked.

"Only one way to find out," Rowan said.

Twenty-eight

"Let's get this straight," Barmy said. "How did you avoid getting crushed by the stone ball?"

"Grr," said Eynek excitedly. "Grr, grr . . . grrr grr grr – grrrrr grr-grrr-grr grr grrr . . . grr . . . grrr grr grrr!"

"He says as the great stone ball drew nearer, the heroic Rowan, using his incredible thief's skills, managed to pick the lock which held the metal shutter shut with the result that the shutter lifted a little and the two intrepid adventurers squeezed through in the nick of time." Ben 's grin faded. "Actually it was touch and go."

"I bet," Barmy said. He was drawing a large circle on the floor beneath the throne, using his stub of chalk. The golden spiders had withdrawn now that someone had agreed to try to resurrect their master, as had the ants, which were wanted by the colony for some more pressing business. But whatever about the ants, Barmy suspected the spiders had not gone far. He could feel their diamond eyes upon him from dark corners of the hall.

He glanced at the emerald tablet. "We need a small, shallow dish. Has anybody got one?"

There was silence for a moment, then Rowan produced a small, shallow dish from the pocket of his jerkin. It was made from gold, encrusted with gems. "I found it," he said sheepishly.

Barmy placed the dish near the edge of the circle and

chalked mystic symbols around it. "Could you wedge a torch between the flagstones there, just there –?" he asked Aspen, pointing. "But don't light it yet."

"Are you sure you know what you're doing?" Lauren said.

"I'm just following the tablet," Barmy told her amiably. The last thing he wanted right now was an argument. He had a strong suspicion that if he could not resurrect King Tarantulus, they would have to contend with every giant spider in the place.

"Mmm," Lauren said suspiciously.

Aspen knelt to drive the torch between the flagstones. "I was thinking, Barmy . . ."

"About the Bong?" Barmy asked. "So was I."

"You don't think . . ."

"I've been almost afraid to think it," Barmy told her frankly. "What do you think?"

"I think we should try," Aspen said.

"Excuse me, Barmy, Asprin, but what are you talking about?"

"Barmy was wondering if we should try to resurrect Lancie, Ben," Aspen said.

"That's a good plan, Asprin. Do you think it will work, Barmy?"

Which was, of course, the $64,000 question. Since he had read the tablet, Barmy had been wondering exactly the same thing himself. He shrugged resignedly and said, "I don't know, Ben. It would be a dreadful disappointment if it didn't work."

"But it would be much worse not to try, Barmy," Ben said reasonably.

And there was no arguing about that. He glanced at Aspen, who nodded. Barmy licked his lips. "We'd have to get him in here – Lancie's body, I mean." He felt his heart thumping and could not control it.

Lauren said, "I think you should try the spell on Lancie first."

"Why do you think that, Lauren?"

"In case it doesn't work," said Lauren bluntly. "At least then we would know what to expect when we try it on King Tarantulus." She looked around them and voiced one of Barmy's current worries. "Because if we can't raise King Tarantulus, his spiders are going to be very angry with us."

"She's right," Aspen agreed.

"The thing is, getting Lancie here might not be all that easy," Barmy said. "We've seen what this place is like for traps." He finished writing on the floor and straightened up. "Besides, I'm not sure I know how to get back to where we left him."

"I do," Rowan said promptly.

"Are you sure?" Aspen asked seriously.

" 'Course I'm sure," Rowan said confidently. "I got here in one piece, didn't I? I reckon if I retrace my steps exactly, I'll know where the traps are. And the spiders seem friendly enough for now."

"For now," Lauren echoed grimly.

"Somebody will have to go with you –" Barmy said.

"Heel, Eynek!" Rowan grinned

"Not just Eynek," Barmy told him. "You'll need somebody to help you with . . . help you with –" He could not bring himself to say *the body*.

"I'll go with you, Rowan," Ben put in. "I can protect you from attack and help you with Lancie. We'd better hurry before he starts to rot."

Barmy closed his eyes and gagged slightly. "Yes, okay," he said.

"Don't start messing about with the spell before we get back," Rowan warned.

"No," promised Barmy, "I won't."

It was not a difficult promise to keep, as it happened, since the full preparations for the resurrection ritual were quite complex. He had to bisect the circle exactly (a task which might have been beyond him had not Lauren come to his aid, sighing) then bisect it again at right angles to form an inner cross. Then he had to draw a second circle, smaller than the first and fill the space between them with more symbols, each one carefully drawn in considerable detail. Finally he had to inscribe two equilateral triangles, one within the other, just outside the circle. More mystic symbols were drawn at the points.

He had just finished the final one when his stub of chalk crumbled into dust and was stretching to ease his cramp when a rumbling sound set him whirling round in panic, reaching for the sword the spiders had taken from him. He noticed Aspen had dropped into a fighting crouch. "I feel naked without my weapon," she murmured.

But they need not have worried. A bizarre sight met their eyes as Eynek entered the chamber, harnessed to a massive golden wheelbarrow. Rowan and Ben had a handle each. In the wheelbarrow lay the mortal remains of Reverend Lancelot Bong, the crossbow bolt still protruding from his chest. With him, locked in their frozen positions, were Pendragon and Facecrusher.

"We had an idea," said Rowan as they trundled to a halt. "What I read of the tablet said it cures paralysis as well as death, so we thought the spell might help these two as well."

"Good idea," said Aspen. She glanced at Barmy. "It is a good idea, isn't it?"

"I think so," Barmy said, although his guess was as good as hers.

"You ready for these three?" Rowan asked.

"Ready as I'll ever be," Barmy muttered. He was finding it difficult to maintain his self control now the body of Lancie was actually in the room. But the preparations were, in fact, complete. There was nothing to be done now except the actual spell.

"Where do you want them?" Rowan asked.

Barmy stared at him blankly for a moment. Should he try the spell on all three at once? Or try them one at a time? He was tempted to go for broke.

"Oh, just put them in the double triangle," he said eventually.

But it was obvious almost at once that all three would not fit. Rowan looked at him for guidance.

"All right," Barmy said. "Can you fit in Facecrusher and Pendragon?"

"I think so."

"Okay, leave Lancie out for the minute."

With Facecrusher and Pendragon in the triangle, Barmy stepped into the circle. "Everybody stand clear," he said, then noticed those of his companions who could move were almost out of sight now, pressed against the chamber walls and hiding behind pillars. They obviously remembered the last time Barmy tried a major spell. That one had been the conjuration of a slith, which brought an entire castle down around their ears.

The resurrection spell was simpler than slith summoning; all the complications and real work were in the preparation. With a last glance at the tablet to remind himself what to do, Barmy closed his eyes, raised both arms above his head, visualized a silver fountain of pure energy erupting upwards from the ground, then began to chant.

"Begoth sumer azram metron hebak!" he intoned. "Slibrah halva benghi corrabana . . ."

It took less than a minute to complete, the newly learned phrases tripping sonorously off his tongue. He opened his eyes again to find Facecrusher and Pendragon stretching. They still looked a bit dazed, but otherwise none the worse for wear. A scattered patter of applause broke out from the edges of the hall.

"Where am I?" Facecrusher asked.

"Can you move out of the triangle, please," Barmy said, wondering if they were really all right.

"Why should I move out of the triangle?" Pendragon asked belligerently, confirming that he, at least, was just the same as ever.

Aspen led them off and Ben and Rowan trotted across to manhandle Lancie's body into the double triangle. They grinned excitedly at Barmy, then trotted off again.

Barmy was feeling far from excited. He was, in fact, more nervous than he had been in years. The spell seemed to have worked on Facecrusher and Pendragon, but their health problems were a lot less extreme than Lancie's. He took a deep breath to still his thumping heart, offered up a quick prayer to whatever gods might possibly be listening and closed his eyes.

"Begoth sumer azram metron . . ." he began.

Even before he finished, he knew it was not going to work. There was no way anybody – let alone Barmy Jeffers – was going to cure a man with a crossbow bolt stuck right through his heart. But he went on anyway, since there was nothing else he could do.

As the last echoes of his chanting died away, Barmy

felt depression sink upon him like a cloud. There was no cheer, no applause. It had not worked. He opened his eyes.

"Will somebody help me get this stupid thing out of my chest?" the Reverend Bong demanded.

Twenty-nine

They were cheering themselves hoarse. Aspen had run across to thump him on the back and Pendragon, fully recovered, was pumping his hand. Barmy felt dazed by unbelief, but there he was, the Reverend Lancelot Bong, complaining bitterly as Ben sat on his chest to pull out the crossbow bolt. It shifted suddenly, then popped like a cork from a bottle. Barmy half expected a fountain of blood, but none came and when, a moment later, the Bong removed his breastplate, there was no sign of a wound. The spell, presumably, was still working – or perhaps wound healing was all part of the magical service.

A movement in the shadows caught his eye and Barmy sobered instantly. "Can you clear the triangle, please," he said urgently. "We have to resurrect the king now. The spiders are getting restless."

They backed away reluctantly, but there was no doubt that behind all the euphoria, they were still in deep trouble. Only Facecrusher, Bong and Pendragon retained their weapons and on their own they could never stave off an attack by the golden spiders – indeed, it was questionable whether the whole party armed to the teeth could stave off an attack by the golden spiders. The creatures were fast, fearless and venomous. It was a difficult combination to defeat.

What would happen, Barmy wondered, if he could not repeat the spell successfully?

He pushed the thought aside and began to mount the

steps to the great crystal throne. The resemblance between King Tarantulus and the mummy in the museum was even more striking close up. Except that Tarantulus somehow managed to look older – far older. Which, Barmy supposed, he was. He found himself trying to remember the age of the Egyptian Pharaoh.

"Here's more statues like the ones in the banquet hall," Rowan called. He had disappeared behind the translucent curtain and was now mingling with the ceramic courtiers.

"Don't touch anything!" Lauren warned. "I don't trust anything in this place."

"Neither do I," agreed Rowan. "Hello, I've found an exit. There's some stairs here, going downwards."

"Can you give me a hand, Ben?" Barmy asked. "And Pendragon and Facecrusher if you're up to it."

He stared into the blank eye-sockets of ancient King Tarantulus. Would the king be grateful for his resurrection? Would he, perhaps, shower Barmy with gifts of gold and jewels? Or would his mind, feeble with age, prove petty and malignant?

Barmy shrugged mentally. He was soon going to find out. Or if he didn't, he was soon going to have big trouble from the spiders.

"Right, Barmy," said Facecrusher briskly, "what do you want us to do?"

"We have to get him into the triangle," Barmy explained. "I thought if I took one arm and Ben the other, you and Pendragon could take a leg each."

"Okay," Pendragon said, without arguing for once. He peered at the figure on the throne. "He doesn't look as though he should be all that heavy."

"What about his gear?" Facecrusher asked. "The sceptre and stuff?"

163

"Yes, we'll leave that by the throne." Gently he removed the filigree crown and eased the sceptre from the leather hand. When he had the valuables placed carefully to one side he said, "Ready?"

"Ready," said Facecrusher.

"Ready," said Pendragon.

"Ready, Barmy," Ben said.

"All together then," said Barmy. He gripped the king's right elbow while Ben gripped the left. "Lift!" he commanded, lifting. The king's arm came away in his hand.

Pendragon and Facecrusher toppled backwards down the steps, each holding an ancient foot. Only the arm Ben gripped seemed to be reasonably anchored, but the entire corpse was now slipping sideways in his direction. Barmy dropped the dismembered member and with a reflex lurch threw his arms around Tarantulus' neck to steady him. The wizened head came away at once, turning as it did so to come nose to nose with Barmy's face.

Revolted, Barmy dropped it, then watched horrified as it bounced down three steps before exploding like a puffball in a cloud of ancient dust. The headless corpse toppled on to Ben, who lost his balance and fell off the dais, taking the remains of the king with him. As they struck the floor, the body too crumbled into dust.

Pendragon picked himself up. "I think," he said glumly, "we've got trouble."

It was the understatement of the century. After a moment of utter stillness, giant spiders began pouring into the throne room from every direction. Nor were they the golden spiders who had carried Barmy, Lauren, Ben and Aspen here: they were huge hairy black spiders, larger and more thickly set than their golden counterparts. Barmy needed no persuasion that these were Tarantulus'

164

soldier spiders, the legions which had kept his realm safe throughout his known lifetime.

"Run!" Facecrusher shouted unnecessarily. She gripped Pendragon by the shoulder. "Come on, Draggie – we'll hold them off while the others get away!"

"Why us?" Pendragon asked.

"We're the ones with swords."

"Oh, yes," Pendragon said. He drew his weapon and hurled himself forward.

Barmy watched Aspen locked in indecision. It was as if he could see what was going through her mind as clearly as if it were a Saturday-night movie. She was unarmed. To tackle the spiders with her bare hands would be utter folly. But she wanted to fight.

"Run!" Barmy roared at her, hoping it might make some difference.

"This way!" Rowan called. "There are no spiders on the stairs!"

Barmy saw Lauren head behind the curtain and disappear among the ceramic courtiers. It was a good move since the spiders seemed to be avoiding that area so far.

Facecrusher and Pendragon closed in on one brute in a pincer movement and hacked at it with their swords. It was a black spider and Barmy noticed it did not move as quickly as the gold variety, although it seemed to have some sort of natural armour, for it was proving very difficult to kill.

There was only one possible course of action – retreat. Aspen had obviously come to the same conclusion, although she turned slowly, as if still half undecided. Eynek appeared out of nowhere and shot past her, heading towards Rowan. Aspen started to run then, only to find herself cut off by two of the very largest spiders.

Barmy grabbed the jewelled sceptre and jumped down from the dais. It was not the best weapon in the world, but it was better than nothing. He lunged forward and brought it down viciously on the back of one of the black spiders that was threatening Aspen. The sceptre jolted so violently that it actually tore from his nerveless hand. The spider did not even turn.

"Tally-ho!" shouted a voice and Barmy saw the Bong surrounded by spiders, spinning on his own axis with a broadsword in both hands. It was an unorthodox strategy, but it seemed to be keeping the brutes at bay.

"You try this, Barmy," Ben called.

Barmy half turned in time to see Ben toss him something. He caught it automatically, then looked at it in amazement. It was the wand that had created the enormous ball which had broken their way into the great cavern in the first place. For the first time since the trouble began in earnest, Barmy felt a flicker of hope. He started to point the wand, then remembered.

"It only works for dwarves, remember?" he shouted, throwing it back to Ben. "You use it!!"

"All right, Barmy," Ben caught the wand.

Barmy turned to see that the spider in front of him had collapsed in a quivering heap. The sceptre had obviously done it far more damage than he thought. He vaulted over the body and grabbed Aspen by the arm. "This way!"

"Thanks, Barmy," Aspen said. She kicked the second spider *en passant* and somehow managed to avoid its lunge.

Together they ran through the curtain, weaving in and out of the frozen courtiers. Out of the corner of his eye, Barmy saw the Bong cut a path through and break into a leaping gallop.

"Ben's about to open up with that blasted wand," he shouted in Aspen's ear.

There was a bright flash and a curiously loud popping noise as a huge ball appeared in the air behind them, then dropped to crush a dozen spiders.

"Way to go, Ben!!" yelled the Reverend Lancelot Bong. "Sock it to them!"

The great ball disappeared quite suddenly and gouts of green fire began to erupt from the wand. Barmy felt a searing heat as one rolled by him no more than a yard away. There were screams behind as spiders began to fry.

"It didn't do that before," he heard Ben say, bewildered. He dropped the wand on the floor, where it began to spin like a firework, throwing flame and lightning everywhere.

Facecrusher and Pendragon began to fight a rearguard action, retreating with sure, synchronized steps.

"Run!" Barmy screamed, which Ben did without a moment's hesitation. Seconds later, Barmy and Aspen were jumping over the spinning wand, followed in a whisker by the Reverend Bong.

"I hope we're not heading for a dead end," Aspen muttered. So did Barmy, though he said nothing.

Dodging around the weird ceramic figures of the courtiers, they reached the stairs and started to run down, but met Lauren running up.

"It's a way out!" she gasped breathlessly. "But there's a grille closing it off. Rowan's trying to pick the lock, but he says he needs more time!"

"We'll hold them off!" Pendragon told her bravely, having arrived on the scene with Facecrusher, who nodded her agreement. They turned, ready to face the foe again.

Barmy glanced behind him. The mass of spiders were closing in. More were dropping down on strands from the ceiling. "You've done enough!" he said. They were both slowing down, their faces moist with sweat.

"Get back to Rowan and tell him we'll hold them off," Barmy instructed Lauren. He grabbed Facecrusher and Pendragon and shoved them after her. "You too. Shout as soon as he's picked the lock."

"You've no weapon!" Lauren said.

"Go!" screamed Barmy, and to his surprise she went. Predictably, Pendragon was not so easy to persuade.

"I don't think –" he began.

"Go!" Barmy screamed again. "We may not be able to hold them off and we'll need somebody to guard the tunnel!"

"Yes, but –"

"Come on, Draggie," Facecrusher muttered, seeing the sense of Barmy's words. She grabbed Pendragon by the arm and tugged him down the stairs.

Barmy turned to find both Lancelot and Aspen hard pressed by more than a dozen of the largest crawlers. They were fighting fiercely, but it was obviously only a matter of time before they went under from sheer weight of numbers.

"Get back!" called Barmy. He ran forward without the least idea what he was going to do.

"We've only just got here!" the Bong called cheerfully. He decapitated a spider with his broadsword.

Mindlessly, Barmy swooped to pick up the spinning wand. Maybe now that Ben had got it started, it would continue to work for him. "Get back!" he screamed again.

"Oh good grief!" he heard Aspen mutter. "He's starting his wretched magic again."

But his move had the desired effect, for they fell back at once. Barmy aimed the wand. It was still spitting green

168

fire, bucking and writhing like a live thing in his hand. He squeezed the end.

The green fire stopped and a fountain of stone balls erupted from the air ahead of him, fortunately travelling outwards towards the spiders. They were not nearly as large as the giant ball which Ben had materialized, but they were large enough and they kept coming, spraying from the wand as if from a machine gun. Several ploughed through the spider ranks, tossing the giant insects aside like rag dolls. But others pounded the pillars, walls and ceiling of the throne room. As more and more pillars smashed to smithereens, there was an ominous rumbling from the ceiling overhead.

"He's doing it again!" yelled Aspen.

He was, too, but somehow he could not stop himself. He stood there, spraying huge stone balls in all directions, listening to the ceiling crack and waiting for the roof to collapse inwards, burying them all. It was a sort of madness, but it was a glorious, exciting madness.

"Drop the wand!" yelled Aspen.

"Whee!" Barmy exclaimed, as happy as he had been when the spider poisoned him. He was drunk with power.

"Come on!" Lancelot Bong shouted. "Rowan's got it open. With any luck we're free and clear."

Still Barmy could not stop.

"*Come on*!!!!" This from Aspen again, desperately.

Ben appeared beside him. "Sorry, Barmy," he said kindly. He bunched one hand into a fist and struck Barmy smartly on the head. Barmy felt the lights go out briefly. Next moment he was hanging across Ben's broad shoulder, nose almost touching the ground, bouncing swiftly towards the stairs and freedom as the roof started to fall in.

Epilogue

"Sorry I lost my head," Barmy said. Even now, long after, he felt exhilarated, but a little guilty.

Aspen shrugged. "If you hadn't, we might all be dead," she said simply. "There were an awful lot of spiders to hold back."

Barmy flushed a little, pleased. They were hanging around in the courtyard of the Monastery of the Benign Immortal, waiting for Lauren, who had taken it into her head to discuss the biochemistry of the ageing process with the Immortal himself. The meeting was taking place in a cell at the back of the monastery. The Immortal, fortunately, had eaten ant food in honour of the occasion and was of normal size again.

Near the gate of the courtyard was a hastily constructed wooden framework, uneasily like a gallows, from which hung a full-sized Möbius loop made from strips of leather. Around it, a group of ancient monks were squabbling about which of them had done most work on it.

"Where is the silly little mm girl?" asked Brother Sunshine testily. "I hate hanging about."

"Here she is now," Barmy said, for Lauren was indeed making one of her grand entrances through an arch, the Benign Immortal on her arm.

"Look at that old fool," whispered Brother Moonbeam, nodding towards the Benign Immortal. "Hasn't the sense of a gnat."

A murmur of agreement swept through the remaining monks, who nonetheless bowed deferentially and applauded as the Benign Immortal came into earshot.

"Have you got his emerald pill, Barmy?" Ben asked. "It's nearly time for the official presentation."

"Tablet," Pendragon corrected him. "It's an emerald tablet."

"It's the same thing, isn't it, Draggie? You *are* stupid."

"I'm not the one who's stupid, Ben," said Pendragon patronizingly. "There are several different usages of the word *tabl*–"

"Oh, stop squabbling, you two," said Aspen irritably. "This is supposed to be a special occasion."

"They can mm-squabble if they like!" Brother Sunshine informed her with equal irritation. "It's very beneficial for the mm-liver."

"For the *liver*?" echoed Brother Moonbeam. "You must be crackers, you stupid, old –"

"Serenity and peace!" exclaimed the Benign Immortal, stopping before Barmy.

"*Serenity and peace!*" intoned the gathered monks.

"Who do they think they're kidding?" Ben asked audibly.

"Give him the tablet," prompted the Reverend Bong in a whisper.

"Oh, sorry," Barmy said. He stepped forward, holding the tablet and launched into his prepared speech. "Revered Immortal, it gives me great pleasure to make this presentation on behalf –"

"Yes, yes," said the Benign Immortal impatiently. He snatched the tablet and peered at it short-sightedly. "It's it! It's it all right! The old death cure on the one side and the transmutation on the other. Hear that?" He raised his

172

voice and looked around triumphantly. "We can turn lead into gold now – we're all going to be rich!"

Barmy expected cheers, but instead the group of monks broke into angry muttering.

"Where are we going to get lead in these stupid mountains?"

"That tablet's fake. That young con merchant made it himself."

"Bet the process is –"

"Who do they think they're –"

"– daft old imbecile doesn't –"

"– expect from a twit who lives in ant hills?"

The Bong cleared his throat loudly and said, "Thank you, friends. Now, if you'll forgive us, the famous emerald tablet retriever and his highly intelligent young sister have to be leaving, so quieten down, otherwise my little friend Ben will set about you with his club."

Silence descended. Barmy hugged Facecrusher and kissed Aspen on the cheek. He shook hands with Pendragon, Ben and Lancie. "Thank you," he said. "Thank you for everything."

"You come back soon, Barmy," Ben told him. He grinned. "Otherwise we'll have to come and get you."

"Grr," said Eynek fondly as Barmy patted him on the head.

He looked round for Rowan and found him. "Good fun, Rowan," he said, smiling sadly.

"Good fun, Barmy," Rowan agreed. He embraced Barmy and pressed something into his hand.

Barmy glanced down to find he was holding a diamond as big as a hen's egg. "I can't take this!" he hissed in a moment of panic. But Rowan only grinned at him.

Lauren, who had missed the transfer, took him firmly by

173

the arm. "Come on," she said. "You're going to have quite enough explaining to do to Mother about where you've been." She smiled at the Benign Immortal. "Goodbye Freddie – nice to have met you."

Freddie? She called the Benign Immortal *Freddie*?

"Goodbye Lauren," said the Benign Immortal. "Hope to see you again." To Barmy he said, "I see you managed to lose your ant armour."

"I –" said Barmy. "I –" But Lauren was half dragging him along. He fell into the familiar contortions of the Quasimodo Walk as they approached the Möbius loop. "Goodbye, everyone," he called, too confused to think of anything more appropriate. "Goodbye. Goodbye."

Horror Classic Gamebooks
by J. H. Brennan

Now you can bring your favourite horror characters
to life in these spinechilling gamebooks.

Dracula's Castle

Deadly traps and evil cunning await Jonathan Harker on
his arrival at the forbidding Castle Dracula. The choice
is yours whether to play the fearless vampire-hunter or
his arch-enemy, the vampire count himself. Will you
have the stamina to survive?

The Curse of Frankenstein

Enter the ghoulish world of Frankenstein and his
monstrous creation. But be warned, you will need skill,
luck and nerves of steel to endure this bloodcurdling
adventure.

Armada

ARMADA

Here are some of the most recent titles in our exciting fiction series:

The Chalet School and Rosalie *Elinor M. Brent-Dyer* £1.75
The Secret of the Forgotten City *Carolyn Keene* £1.95
The Masked Monkey *Franklin W. Dixon* £1.95
The Mystery of the Creep-Show Crooks *M. V. Carey* £1.95
Horse of Fire *Patricia Leitch* £1.75
Cry of a Seagull *Monica Dickens* £1.75
The Secret of Moon Castle *Enid Blyton* £1.95
Legion of the Dead *J. H. Brennan* £1.95

Armada paperbacks are available in bookshops and news-agents, but can also be ordered by post.

HOW TO ORDER

Please send the purchase price plus 22p per book (maximum postal charge £3.00) to Armada Paperbacks, Cash Sales Dept., GPO Box 29, Douglas, Isle of Man. Please use cheque, postal or money order – do not send currency.

Name (BLOCK LETTERS) ....

Address ....

....

....

While every effort is made to keep prices low, it is sometimes necessary to increase them at short notice. Collins Children's Books reserve the right to show new retail prices on covers which may differ from those previously advertised in the text or elsewhere.